James Locke

Tweed and Don

Or Recollections and Reflections of an Angler for the Last Fifty Years

James Locke

Tweed and Don
Or Recollections and Reflections of an Angler for the Last Fifty Years

ISBN/EAN: 9783337107192

Printed in Europe, USA, Canada, Australia, Japan

Cover: Foto ©Andreas Hilbeck / pixelio.de

More available books at **www.hansebooks.com**

TWEED AND DON;

OR,

RECOLLECTIONS AND REFLECTIONS OF AN ANGLER

FOR THE LAST FIFTY YEARS.

The magic wand then let us wield,
For ance that five-and-forty speeld,
See crazy, weary, joyless eild,
Wi' wrinkled face,
Comes hosten-hirplin owre the field,
Wi' creepin' pace.

EDINBURGH:
WILLIAM P. NIMMO, 2, ST DAVID STREET.
LONDON : SIMPKIN, MARSHALL, AND CO.

MDCCCLX.

Like Junius, I dedicate this little Book to

The Public.

I did not think, when I wrote it for my Sons, 'away
from the din and turmoil of London' (to be laid by for
some future time), that I should so soon see it in print.
This has been solely at the request of a friend who is not
an angler.   As I owe no man anything but love, I hope
they will temper any observation they may perhaps make
on it with the same virtue ; and

I remain,

Their most obedient Servant,

JAMES LOCKE.

119, REGENT STREET, LONDON.

Contents.

⁓≼≽⁓

INTRODUCTION.

Longa Captamus Arundine Praedas.

Y DEAR BOYS,—I have often thought of writing, for your amusement, a short account of my fishing in the neighbourhood of Edinburgh, that, if you are spared, you may remark the difference which manufactories and drainage have made there, on the rivers and waters I frequented in my youth. I will also extend the circle to other places; and though of late there has been much written and said on the Art of Angling (it being almost a fashion to do so), I think, as it is now fifty years since I first took to it, I can tell you something that you will not find in any of the books which have been published on this pleasant sport. Now, I

do not write to you as novices, or as not knowing
anything about it; for I suppose you heartily
interested in the subject, and as having read up
to it from Lady Juliana Berners, down to
Hofland, Stoddart, Younger, Stewart, Ephemera,
etc., and also the Border Angler, or British
Railway Streams. I propose to give you a little
more practical detail of how to *get* and *keep* the
Stone or May-fly, Partail and Creeper, for your
baits; and I hope I shall be able to add to your
amusement and your knowledge, by detailing
what I have really experienced myself at different
places.

Beginning, therefore, with the days when I
was young, and before I took my departure to
the Great Metropolis, I shall conduct you, and
those who may please to read, to many a pleasant
river which I have visited, both for sport and
health, since that time. The details I will not
make long, but will only give a few practical
rules, that, when you or others go to a river, you
may not be disappointed altogether from not
knowing when to fish, and what trout and
salmon are likely to take in the different states

of thc waters. And I hope I may lead you, while fishing, to think of greater things than the mere sport of killing fish, and to learn that he is a happy man who can at times shake off the world and its cares; and with a contented mind, and a heart grateful for mercies received, enjoy all things in his *great Father*, and be happy and delighted whenever

HE GOES A-FISHING.

J. L.

THORNILEE-ON-TWEED, 19*th Nov.* 1859.

NEIGHBOURHOOD OF EDINBURGH.

Lochend.

MY cheerful home, from 1808 to 1819, was at the bottom of a sweet hawthorn lane, leading from Leith Walk to the Quarry Holes, now quite changed from its once bridle lane appearance by walls of stone and lime. It was generally called Lovers' Lane, for its beauty and its solitude. It was quite destroyed when a quarry of whinstone, to pave the road between Leith and Edinburgh, for the first time was opened near to the top of it. 'Twas here that I first took up the rod and bent my way over to the loch, which I could trace from my bed-room window, and at that time full of good large perch. Sometimes, very early in the fine mornings of May and June, I would scramble over hedges and ditches, straight as the crow flies, in the company of my companion, Thomas Campbell, who had to return to his work at Marshall's at six A.M. Marshall was a marble-cutter in Leith Walk, and was engaged at that time in sculpturing the two figures which now adorn the front of the Bank of Scotland in Edinburgh ; they occupied him for three years, and he shed tears when they were sent away. T. C. became a sculptor in London, and died in 1858. The only bait we took was worms, dug from the garden the night before. The perch is a greedy and a foul-feeding fish, and will take anything, even the entrails of its fellows. Many were the good perches we took in this way; and I used sometimes to kill them freely with live minnows, when I managed to obtain a few from some of my school-fellows, who fished them out of Canonmills Loch ; and, just fixing them dead or alive on one of my large bait-hooks, we often got them ¾lb. and upwards. As an instance of voraciousness in the perch, I may here mention, that one morning, my friend hooked one with the worm, which, on dragging out, he found to be in reality two. A perch, about 1½ lbs., had endeavoured, perhaps the day before, to devour .

a small one ; but, in the act, the large back-fin
of the latter had stuck in the mouth of the de-
vourer, and had choked him. The small one,
however, nothing deterred while carrying about
its incubus, had caught at the bait ; and when
drawn out of the water, my friend found, that
although the small one was still alive, the large
one had been dead some time. O how delightful was early morn by this Loch ! I have been
on its banks at three in the morning; and occasionally, as I would cast up my eyes to Arthur's
Seat, I have seen the shepherd driving his flocks
before him on the fine green sward slanting
down from the upland ridge, the sun glinting
its most cheerful rays over the distant heights
and the ranges of the Pentlands ; Scotia's dar-
ling seat lying before me in all the majesty of
silence,—no smoke as yet from any of its house-
hold fires—no tall chimneys pointing to the skies
and vomiting black smoke, which we now see in
this view—the debris from Salisbury Crags
making that beautiful reposing angle so much
admired—the sound of St Giles' striking the
hours, and the Tron Kirk swearing that the tale
was true. We often came away about six
o'clock, with eight or nine good perch strung on

a string. Although Duddingstone Loch could have been fished in the same way, we seldom went to it ; when we did so, we were not successful, although both pike and perch were often taken in it. There is still fishing in both places : but in walking over the sides of Lochend the other day, I found it much altered. One or two of the large stones on which we stood sometimes, and threw the perches out over our heads, like podlies at the end of Leith Pier, still remain.

Coltbridge,

NEAR EDINBURGH, RIVER LEITH.

To this pleasant little village I often went on the Saturday afternoons, and sometimes after eight o'clock in the summer evenings, to fish with fly in the Water of Leith, killing trout above and below the bridge. I remember catching a large eel with my fly,—a rather rare occurrence ; and, wasting all my cast line in the dark, had to give it up, not having been possessed of a second. Many a good trout have I seen taken with a very small fly, thrown from the corner above the

bridge at the tail-stream of Dalry Mills; and
many a good trout with set lines have I pulled
out in the morning, in the garden on the other
side. But now the lime which is used at the
mills of Gorgie and other places, with the smallness of its waters from drainage and other causes,
make sport at an end here. There is no such
thing as a trout to be had, and little done even
at Currie and Colinton. Eels have often been,
and are still, an object of curiosity; and in this
Water of Leith, I remember, one day in July or
August 1812, being at the back of Bonnington
distillery fishing for eels, where one time they
were plentiful, that, watching under the stump
of an old *saugh* tree, I observed little bunches of
hair-like threads come up to the surface of the
water, and, as I looked, they separated and became little eels. This I have often mentioned;
but my piscatory friends only shake their heads.
However, I maintain to this day, that they were
young eels just emerging into life. I watched
them while they did so, and viviparous I always
believed them to be; for I could no more be
mistaken, than that horse-tail hairs could turn
into *flukes*.

Musselburgh.

Within these twenty-five years I have taken a good basket of yellow trout about a mile above the town, and beyond Inveresk, and before you come to some Policies, as they are called. There is still some sea-trout fishing above the old bridge, and also near the sea, though not much frequented, and almost never but in a flood.

Roslin Castle.

One of our great days was to the Esk at this place, after long looking and longing for the fastday or other holiday. I have seen four or five of us boys start for it, after buying a hook or two from Somerville's in Leith Street; the kind old gentleman—for all the shopkeepers there were then gentlemen—giving us some good instructions how to throw our lines without *sleeching* off our hooks. Proceeding by the North Bridge at early day, how sweet was the scent of the peppermint from the gardens below! How different now! .Where were once beautiful, dark-green beds of this plant, we now see, puffing and belching, steaming railway engines. Continuing our way through Buccleuch Pend, and along by the Meadows and the Sciennes, we pass the Grange Toll, the Pow Burn, and on to Burdiehouse by the Windmill and St Catherines. This burn then ran in many a zigzag course. What beautiful red trout were once its inhabitants! Where are they now? Its bed is now cut straight: its waters are gone, and so are they!

We got to the Castle, then to the Linn below the paper mill. Some *sleech* off their hooks at the first throw, and their sport is at an end for the day. I succeed in getting two or three beautiful trouts, of half a pound each; others get glorious nibbles; and we trudge into Edinburgh, quite happy with our sport, short as it was, and hungry as hawks. Ah! how happy is the angler! as Sir Thomas More says, 'If his sport should fail him, he at the least hath his holsom walk, and, mery at his ease, a swete ayre of the swete savour of the meade of flowers that maketh him huugry: he heareth the melodious harmonie of fowles; he seeth the young swans, herons, ducks, cotes, and many other fowles.'

I am told, if you fished there now, you would be gazed at,—all the trout having been destroyed by lime, and other deleterious matter, long since.[1]

I remember an old ash tree at Dryden, near Roslin, which my father felled, and for which he gave L.37, 15s.,—some *goodly sticks or stycks* in Scotland, though Dr Johnson saw none.

Glencorse.

I went once in 1817, with my lamented and dear friend George Brunton, who afterwards became editor of the *Patriot* newspaper in Edin-

[1] The Duke of Buccleuch is reported to have said, at a meeting of Commissioners of Supply of Water at Edinburgh in 1858, speaking of preserving the rivers pure, ' That Hawick, Selkirk, and Galashiels, under the pressure of the Tweed Commissioners, had made arrangements by which the water was so filtered, that the poisonous ingredients were prevented getting into the river.' This is a dream of his Grace. I never saw such: there is no such thing. At Galashiels and Selkirk, no doubt, such a thing ought to be done, and has been long talked about. —A company a few years ago tried this on the Don ; but failed to make it pay.

burgh, and others, to fish here; but, alas! when
we got there, I could only see some small trouts,
which fled from us, as Rodger said of Jenny, as
from a 'shelly-coated cow.' We visited the
Crawley springs, at that time only bubbling out
of the ground in two or three places, not yet
having been taken care of by the Water Company; nor were there as yet any Compensa-
tion Ponds in this neighbourhood. The day
turning wet, and our habits being social, we all
went to an honest ale-house for cakes and
ale. The youths of Edinburgh at that time
never met together but they discussed something. There was little conversation then in
Scotland at table, but plenty of discussion,
and in Edinburgh, society to this day, as I
find it, *they are tarred wi' the same stick.* Our
subject got soon as obscure as Milton's devils
did on the Lake of Fire when they discussed
theology. Brunton was very eloquent; and,
when we got up to go, he was nowhere to be
found, and we had to take the road without
him. He soon after came up with us. He
had stepped into the churchyard, which was
adjacent, and had written the following lines
on the tombstone of his grandfather, which he

gave me in remembrance of the day; beginning thus :—

> By the grave of my fathers I'll set me a while,
> And think of the men who, released from their toil,
> Nor sigh for life's pleasures, nor weep for its sorrow,
> Whose days are all joy, and who fear no to-morrow.
> All around me is still, not a zephyr is stirring;
> > All is mute save the sheep, which now bleat on the
> > hill,
> And the croon of the muircock, which round me is
> > whirring:
> > All is awfully desolate, silent, and still.
> > > Etc.   Etc.

Lasswade.

I saw, in 1818, a trout caught in the garden behind Muir's Inn, which weighed five pounds. From all I know, it was the last of this poisoned race in this place. Mark this, ye polluters and defilers of pure streams. I have also fished for trout at Melville Castle, and, along with my father, chased many from stone to stone at Dalhousie; but 'the place that once knew them, knows them no more.'

FISHING.

1. Pectoral Fin.   3. Anal Fin.   5. Dorsal Fin.
2. Ventral (or Belly). 4. Back Fin.   6. Tail.

They spawn about October and November; are in perfection in May and June.

DESCRIPTION (AS MENTIONED BY STODDART).

Salmo Ferox of Lochawe.
Salmo Fario, common Trout.
Gillarious Trout (Gizzard).
Salmo Cæcifer or Levenensis.
Salmo Salar (the Salmon).

Trout Fly-Fishing.

THIS is decidedly the favourite mode of fishing in Scotland; and, when about to exercise it, the first step taken is to get a ROD of about thirteen feet, or longer if

you can wield it, and light, so as you can
handle it with ease with one hand. There are
not now, as formerly, any great favourites in
the fraternity of rodmakers, such as Chevalier,
of Bell Yard, Fleet Street, who has been dead
many a day. Eaton and Bernard are equally
good, and such of the fishing-rod makers in
Edinburgh as can keep good seasoned wood for
the materials. They have rods at all prices,
according as they are mounted and finished,
from 15s. to 35s. I prefer one in two pieces,
and spliced; or in three pieces,—the part next
the but-end only in a ferrule, the top of cane,
tied together with pretty fine twine well waxed.
I have seen some rods made from bamboo cane
by De Masser, a Frenchman; but they are
wretched tools.

LINE.—Thirty yards of this, either in hair,
or silk and hair, or any other kind thin and
solid, as it casts better if a little wind, on a
good sized reel or winch pretty large in the
round; or you may wind on any old line or
fine cord, and, when nearly full on, the reel
will more quickly wind up and run out. Let
it taper as fine as you can get it, so as to join
in well with your cast-line—' small by degrees,

and beautifully less'—to the fly. I seldom fish with more than two. Much has been said about killing trout with one hair; but I don't mean to try it, and I do not recommend it. Fine gut can now be got in Church Passage, Piccadilly, as fine as any Flanders mare's tail I ever saw.

BOOK OF FLIES.—Many gentlemen carry large assortments. I do not approve of this, as they get old, and the gut gets dry. The moth gets into your book also, without great care; carry a little tobacco-leaf in it. The irons also get rusty, as you occasionally take out your book in a shower of rain. Now, I am one of those who think there is a great deal too much said and fuss made, about flies. I have seen every kind of fly kill in the same hour and in the same day, sometimes four or five of us fishing rivers and streams with all colours and sizes of hooks. I prefer the March-dun, a red hackle, or a yellowish or brown fly, like the Professor, and a palmer or two. More fish with large flies than with small ones. A prevailing notion, especially among beginners, is, that fish do not see them;—not a greater mistake. Trout, I have no doubt, see every

minute thing that comes across the stream; and
you can seldom fail when you fish with the
smallest flies. Your book, of course, must contain a small hank of gut, a few yards of string,
cobbler's wax, a good needle or two, some fine
whity-brown thread, a pair of scissors, large-eyed
for the fingers, a good knife, a coil or two of
different-coloured silk, and a dozen or two of
different-sized hooks, which I prefer all of the
round bend. As I proceed, you may see how all
these may be wanted at the water-side.

BAG, BASKET, AND BOOTS.—Some prefer a
bag, as easier carried : but your fish are apt to
get heated in it; and I therefore always prefer a moderate-sized basket, made of the common willow wand. If you wade,—to me the
most delightful thing in the summer-time,—put
on boots well nailed or tacketed, and worsted
stockings or socks; trousers rather long,—they
thus prevent in some measure small gravel from
getting in if you wear shoes. Carry a dry pair
of shoes and stockings; besides the comfort,
cold is thus prevented. I prefer to have
very *small* holes in the upper leathers of my
shoes or boots for wading, that the water may
run freely out. Prevent as much as possible

sand from getting in. If you are to wade deep,
you must have waterproofs and boots accordingly; but these more properly belong to salmon-
fishing.

COAT.—The drab colour is the best for
standing the sun's rays, as heather mixtures
soon lose their colours in summer. Let it not
be too light in colour. That which Lord Elcho
is now introducing for rifle corps is a capital
colour for fishing in ; and, at a great distance,
the figure of a man glides, like the witches in
Macbeth, 'into thin air ;' and I have heard
a celebrated trout-fisher say, that on the days
he fished with a shepherd-plaid dress or a light
drab hat, he never killed many. Its fabric
should be such as not to let the flies always
stick into it,—a very great nuisance oftentimes
in a wind or walking over your ground ; also
rather thick than thin ; for, at the water-side, it
is better to be warm than cold ; and, if the day
be warm, you can leave off your waistcoat. I
prefer a Tweed hat to a cap when' fishing, as it
is best for twisting your leash of flies round it.

FLASK.—Small and sparingly used ; just a
little sip after coming out of the water, which
warms and does you good, but never more at a

time than what Mynheer van Dunk allowed of
water to his brandy; and we know this was
just as much as is to be found on the leaves of
the rose in a dewy morning.

SMALL POCKET TESTAMENT,—which you
will find great satisfaction in, while you read a
parable (which I believe to be all true instances.
Our blessed redemption would not be advanced
by fiction), or commit to memory a short cardi-
nal point, to the solace of your minds, when you
shelter yourselves from a shower under some
overhanging rock, or from the noontide sun
beneath the umbrage of a leafy tree;—a small
one being easily carried in your side-pocket.
The Puritan fathers were wont to carry the
whole Book with them. It was a small thick
volume, called an 18mo size, and was sometimes
found in collections of old books in St Mary's
Wynd, Edinburgh, or the Strand, London,
under the name of the Cromwell Bible.

And now, when you find yourself all equipped
for your sport, the weather may be unpropitious.
There is not, dear readers, bear in mind, at all
seasons, a more uncertain sport than fishing.

The Vale of Gala.

HIS Vale was once designated by a face-
tious friend of mine as "a lang road by
the side of a burn between twa hills;" but
what a change has come over it now! The rail-
road winds through it, and it is no more a lang
road. Supposing you have taken your seat in
the carriage, do not, gentle youths, stray in
pleasure-paths, and turn aside to minor waters
about Tynehead or Heriot, but go on gladly
and rejoicingly with an honest and a cheerful
heart, the characteristics of a true angler; for
when oiled with these,

> ' The wheels o' life
> Gae down hill scrievin
> Wi' rattling glee.'

And so will you find the wheels of the railway
from Tynehead to Stow, where you may stop
and begin your sport. But, before you begin,
please to cast your eyes up to a fine, sub-
stantial building, which Alexander Mitchell,
Esq., of Stow, has lately built—a town-house,

and which, I am told, contains reading-rooms
and library for the working-classes. How is
it that this class say they are not cared for?
Never since Adam's transgression have they
been more so than at the present time; and is
not the structure before you a beautiful instance of watchfulness over their comforts?—
throwing, as it were, an arch of mutual connection between rich and poor; giving them
the means of cultivating their minds, the noblest
of the desires of our common nature, and endeavouring to make those of his estate and
hamlets an intellectual and intelligent people.
The poet Gray pathetically laments in the
'Elegy,' that in his day the ploughman and
woodman—the rude forefathers of the hamlet
—had gone to their narrow cells quite neglected
in this respect:—*Then*

> ' Knowledge to their eyes her ample page,
> Rich with the spoils of time did ne'er unroll.'

Now we see a glorious change. In many
other places,—Peebles, for instance,—we also
see gentlemen associating together for their
people's good, and for the supply of their wants,

bodily and spiritually,—men who hold their being on the terms,

> ' Each aid the others.'

Burns adds,

> ' Come to my bowl, come to my arms,
> My friends and brothers,'

and so do I take them to mine.

But you have now put up your Rod and are ready, having ascertained that the water is in good fishing order,—for it is of no use to come on these occasions a fool's errand. Say it is now about the end of April, and the song of the Yellow Haired Laddie comes across your mind ; or, perhaps, those of the greatest pastoral in the English language, as Campbell calls it, ' The Gentle Shepherd,' so little read now a days.

> ' This sunny morning Rodger cheers my blood,
> And puts a' nature in a cheerful mood.
> How lightsome its to see the rising plants,
> To hear the birds chirm o'er their pleasant rants.'

Now, my certy, you have done well, one-and-a-

half dozen of trout. You see, casting at right
angles across the stream, is the way to kill trout,
notwithstanding all that is said to the contrary.
The water is of a a light porter colour; had it
been otherwise, casting *fine* and *far* would have,
no doubt, been best; and had it been a low water,
and of course clear, to cast up the water would
have been the plan. It is no new thing to do
this. I remember, twenty-five years ago, being
at Kelso, either at William Pyles' back-room, or
at the Cross Keys, my old friend Yule's, a dis-
sertation on fishing began among a few who
were ' moistening their clay,' and, after much
said by two who seemed to know well about it,
the whole argument came to short strokes;
and, like the story in Blackwood, how many
fins has a cod—at a word. Do you fish up the
water or down the water?—at a word; down
the water was answered; and he was immediately pronounced to be no fisher. Having
taken your luncheon at two o'clock, and fished
down near to the cauld leading to the first
woollen mills, and up again to Bowland
station, you get home by the 6.30 train to
your ' ain fire-side.' This you may occasionally repeat, and, according as the water is low

or high, minnow, partail, worm or creeper, may
be used. I shall begin with the two first of
these baits; but, in the first place, I must say
something of the capital of this district, now
the Leeds, I may say, of Scotland; as I have
promised not only to discourse of fish and their
various lures, but to add to your knowledge in a
kind of 'etchings by the way,' here a little and
there a little. But I will begin first at Inverleithen, and then come down to the flourishing
town of Galashiels.

Inberleithen or Innerleithen.

Sweet be thy name in my remembrance.
'Twas here that I spent many happy days—alas,
never more to return,—still I give thanks for all
I have had and enjoyed in this place—Its
pastoral valleys by the Leithen; the banks of
the Tweed, its classic ground; the 'Bonny
Bush Aboon Traquair,' of which you see the
remains on the opposite side, reminding you of
that beautiful song of Allan Ramsay, and its
plaintive air, adapted by Boildieu, in his introduction or overture to his opera of 'La Dame

Blanche.'[1]   There is here good accommodation
at Riddle's Inn, and, if the angler is desirous of
staying a week or two in this celebrated water-
ing place, there are plenty of good lodgings to
be had in the village, said to be the St Ronan's
Well of Sir W. Scott's Novel. But to confine
myself to fishing operations : we have the pool,
at the confluence of the Leithen and Tweed,
then the Weaver's pool, a right good salmon
one. The trout fisher must not pass over the
water between these two pools, without giving
the trout a call. The next salmon pool is Juniper
Bank, then the Bar pool—capital at some times
for both salmon and trout. There are some
good pools on the estate of Mr Ballantyne of
Hollylee, which, in compliance with his polite
notice requesting no angler to fish opposite his
house, you should pass over quickly. Although,
had I been a country gentleman, lonely, and
gazing at times out on the river, I would have
been but too happy to see a few honest anglers
at their sport. Conforming to his request, you
pass on, and the next pool for trout and salmon

---

[1] In 1837 I took a bit of this old bush. It is now, I
am told, all gone and decayed ; but a new bush is planted
in the same place.

is Howgate, at Thornilee, in the parish of Innerleithen, and county of Selkirk. All the while
you are coming down from Innerleithen you
have the celebrated Ettrick Forest on the south
side of the river, which extends from this to the
Yarrow, famous in story and in Scottish song;
and, no doubt, in anticipating some old feud of
the border—one of them runs thus,

> ‘ Sister, sister, I dream’d a dream,
>   I hope it won’t breed sorrow ;
>   I dream’d that your true love and mine,
>   Lay sleeping sound on Yarrow.’

This is on the estate of Stow, and the lands are
farmed by Mr Roxburgh, who can cast a capital
line for salmon, for I never saw him descend to
trout. Next is Elibank Boat Pool for trout.
The old castle, the scene of the story of Muckle
Mouth’d Meg, stands just above the house where
the late Eagle Henderson lived, and few ever
spent an evening with him that soon forgot it,

> ‘ Ah ! memory, whither art thou straying? ’

I well remember spending an evening here, and
when put ashore, as I supposed, on the bank, I
stepped up to the middle in Tweed. Below

this, the Island Stream, the Knout Seg, followed
by the Steel pool, all of which are good for trout
and salmon. Then comes the famous pool of
Gleddis Wiel, where Laidlaw, Hogg, and Sir
Walter, used to liester salmon, and which is so
well and graphically described by Lockhart in
his Life of Scott, and also in the Border Angler,
page 67, that I must pass it. This sport in
Tweed must now, in the words of Pope, only
'Live in description and look green in song;'
for, by the new law of the Duke of Roxburghe,
it is prohibited; but, as an old fisher, I have
been a partaker of its excitement and also of
its sport; for, by the old law, it was allowed so to
do by night or day; and I well remember
when my jolly friend Bryson came out on a
geological excursion to the Quarry, being accompanied by him to Clapperton's Haugh, and
on throwing a noble shaft at a fish, I was nearly
swept away in the flood, having struck it in too
deep and rapid water; and, on recovering myself,
saw a fine salmon of 25 to 30 lbs. walloping
at the end of my liester down stream. It was
found next morning by one of the hinds, and a
good prize it was. In summer I have seen
great sport here with the *liester*, when the river

ran low and clear. This is reckoned one of the best pools on this water. Many a good run I have got myself, and many as capital have I been witness to. The last good one I saw about twelve years ago; I offered the old man 5s. for the fish while on the line, and to take my chance of his landing it. He said little, for I never saw a more exciting run; the whole of his line out, and the fish 'scudding under favouring gales,' many yards sometimes over the very top of the water, and the line meanwhile not being seen; when landed, for I gaffed it myself, I renewed my offer with addition, but the old man resisted, shook his head, and said 'Na, I'll just een tak it hame and let the guidwife see't.' It proved to be a buttoner[1] fish of twenty pounds. Where are such fish now? Echo answers, where! The next stream which can be fished from the side, after you pass the Hurl, is immediately opposite the Cottage. This modest dwelling, the scene of many a blythe night of meeting, has been the place of rendezvous of an old fishing club these thirty years bygone; and of all places for a fishing station it is one of

---

[1] These buttoner fish are so called from an exterior mark, like a button, on their throat.—' *Grey Schule* ' *fish.*

the best and most convenient, a good trouting
stream being only a rod's length from the door.
Moreover, while you take your "ease in your
Inn," or rest your head on your pillow, you can
behold the state of the water, which, in an unpropitious morning for sport is no doubt very
agreeable ; for a 'little more sleep a little more
slumber,' after a hard day previously at the
water is sometimes pleasant. Here have I seen
come, with faces blanched like a London baker,
those who had been confined for months to the
desk or counter, and go away in a few days
with the blush of the rose on their cheek. I
have seen grief personified, depart smiling and
cheerful ; and have I not seen also avaricious
hearts enter, and go out again resolving for
the future to be more beneficent ! So much
for our Cottage at the Quarry.[1] Oh that

[1] Here in the spring we are visited by many cuckoos,
and Shortrede, the shepherd, told me a curious story
about one ; it had laid an egg—as they generally do,—in a
small bird's nest, on the hill, and when the young cuckoo
was hatched along with the rest, by its size and strength
of wing, it turned out all the other little ones from the
nest. He often put these in again, and the old pair had
great difficulty to keep them all in food. But one
morning, he found the little brood had been uncere-

those once so happy here were permitted to revisit this peaceful and humble abode! How pleased would we be to see their happy faces, and to repeat over again many of our curious tales relating to fishing—many a time, and oft, told with great glee and fun. The old poet says somewhere, that the joys we have enjoyed the gods cannot deprive us of; and as I would rather leave melancholy reminiscences, I shall pass downwards to the Caddonlee Water, on the estate of Admiral Pringle, just now no more. The first pool on this water is the Rampling, from the number of ramps, or wild onions, which grow abundantly on the south side. The Ashiestiel boat pool,—on the side of which you see the oak tree (not a huge tree), where, we are informed by Lockhart, Sir Walter Scott sat often while he was composing Marmion—The Gullets at the Bridge, Moss, and Nedpath pools, follow, the last of which is on Fairnilee water, the property of Mrs Pringle of Haining. Near this picturesque bridge is the Nest, where a club

moniously turned out by it, and all lay dead on the ground. The young cuckoo was shortly afterwards sent to Edinburgh, in a cage, where, however, it soon after followed them to the grave.

or company of gentlemen meet for fishing and
shooting; and, as it is expressed by one of them,
'Here kindred spirits resort.' They have now
a long stretch of water, extending from Thornilee to Ettrick foot,—and much amusing and intelligent conversation have I enjoyed at their
hospitable table, some of their members being
much skilled in Tweed fishing matters. (See
Mr Russell's examination on the last Tweed
Bill). They have lately printed a limited number
of a small volume of songs or happy memories,
which contains some pretty engravings by
Forrest, of the different places of interest adjacent to their fishings, and I will end this short
sketch, with extracting one which I think good,
and it is, no doubt, the index of a fine mind.

I'd be an Angler, born near a river,
　Nightly its murmurs would lull me asleep;
Daily its banks I'd be roving for ever,
　Enticing the bright ones that gleam in the deep.
I'd never care for city-bred pleasures,
　Seeking for mine where the gentle waves leap :
I'd be an Angler, watching my treasures,—
　The sportive and bright ones that gleam in the deep.

My magical wand would be gift of a fairy,
　Her's, too, my hooks with their beautiful wings;

And she'd spin me a line of that stuff light and airy,
　That over her bower the gossamer flings.
Oh! then for the trout so watchful and wary!
　Each summer-day's ramble a basketful brings:
I'd be an Angler in league with a fairy,
　And lodge in a bower where the sweet linnet sings.

But were this denied me, and each finny rover
　Were shy as a maiden when lovers draw near,
Surely 'tis better, ere life's dream is over,
　To angle in hope, tho' hope disappear.
Oh! Winter will come, and too soon discover
　That Angling, like life, must draw to a close;
But who would not Angle on, just like a lover,
　And heed not the thorn when in view of the rose.

Now, although all this water is good for both
trout and salmon fishing with the rod,—for I
never saw a net or coble above Kelso,—yet it
is not so well adapted for the spawning of
salmon, as those fine streams with small round
gravel bottoms, which lie from four to ten miles
above. There are some fine streams between
Innerleithen and Peebles; and, on a space of
water, say a distance of one mile, I have counted,
on one side alone, ten or twelve redds. To
those who know little of this most interesting
part of natural history, I would wish to explain,

that these are the places where salmon spawn,
where the run is a gentle ripple, but not deep,
with fine gravel ; and where a shade of any bush
or tree overhangs ; there, most likely, you will see
them busy,—you will observe the gravel as if
newly turned up. In fact, the male fish is provided by nature, at this season, with a bony
substance or *kip*, which grows on his lower
jaw, to enable him to make the hole in the
gravel for the female to deposit her spawn in ;
and further in the upper jaw, it also has a hole,
into which, when its mouth is closed, it exactly
fits—this bony substance falls off, they say, with
the season, as they are seldom found with it when
quite clean or new from the sea. I quite believe,
from long observation and study of their habits,
that, although generally seen in pairs on the
redds, that the spawn or ova is impregnated by
coition, having observed them from a tree, make
a great plunge toward each other in the stream,
and the male fish *strike her ;* and it may be that
all her ova may be impregnated at one time ; and
I have often seen the female fish spawning, and
no male fish near her.[1] No doubt, ova can be

[1] I have been told that Greenland fishers have observed
whales sport thus ; but this is—very like a whale.

carried to different places, and impregnated by milt, as we know has been done by Shaw and others, as the female does not deposit all her spawn on one redd ; and, at the same time, I have little doubt, that intercourse with the male takes place between the intervals of spawning. On this much debated question, I must note what Mr Younger says, 'If we have no proper idea of the purpose of the large kip or pike, like a finger, growing in projection from the under snout of the male salmon, just previous to the spawning time or season, and fitting into a hole of proper dimensions on the upper chap of the snout, and this pike falling off so suddenly and entirely, and its case also filling up immediately after spawning, need we wonder that the still more complex construction of the organs of generation and of the manner of their use, should, to this day, be unascertained.' This was written some twenty years ago, I think. I must mention that the Tweed is more and more frequented by the bull-trout, which, to all appearance, is a salmon, but of a coarser spotted kind of fish. The smolts of this fish have grey fins,—the sea-trout, orange,—the salmon, black fins ; but, in the present Act, there is no mention of the smolt, therefore, young fishers may kill them without molestation from the water bailiffs.

Galashiels.

There is little doubt that in early days these were the Shiels of Gala, or the lonely huts of a great stretch of pastoral country; and, being in the neighbourhood of plenty of wool, the inhabitants took to the spinning of it and weaving it into a coarse kind of cloth of the district,— Galashiels grey, and latterly, Galashiels blue, being well known. In 1809, I remember piece after piece of these colours, coming in alternately per carrier, to make our best suits for Sunday. Soon after, a little foreign wool was beginning to be used; but, I well remember, say five years before this, of being here, and there were none of these tall chimneys, which we see now, some having sprung up, with gourdish quickness; and the names of steam or gas were not known in all its borders. But the shepherd's plaid, or more properly the maud the herdsman used to wear, in all the upper wards, Selkirk, Roxburgh, Galloway, Dumfries, and Ayr, was adopted by some gentlemen for trousers, very likely by Sir W. Scott, who lived near, and also by Lord Brougham, who wore this check. In 1832 or 1834 a fashion set in for this article, without precedent in Scotch manufacturing history. The black-and-white check getting introduced to the Oxford and Cambridge men, it became universally worn in a very short time; but, changes are lightsome, and a desire for other colours of the same texture and material took place, and brown-and-drab Tweels, often written in the invoices to the Londoners, Twee^d, which was meant to be Tweelds; the word Tweed came to be the common name of all this class of goods; but the maud, from which the whole of this idea came, well deserves a little digression, as Swift says:—

THE SHEPHERD'S MAUD.—The maud may be said to be a long scarf, from 3 yards to 4½ yards long, generally 1½ yard wide, and sometimes 2 yards; the most common colour is the check of six threads of black and six of white, known technically as a six-and-six check, called the Lowland or Border check; and, in the counties of Northumberland, Cum-

berland, Roxburgh, and Dumfries, when a shep-
herd-boy first goes 'to service out amang the
farmers roun,' the 'gudewife' cuts a 'whang,'
of about three or four yards length, from
her home-spun plaiden web, to keep him warm
when herding the sheep on the hills. As the
youth grows and gets bigger, the maud which
has been thus homely made, is, of course, in-
creased in size. Accordingly, in M'Neil's song
of 'The Plaidy,' we have the following line,—

'There's room in't, dear lassie, believe me, for twa.'

But although the black-and-white check is that
generally worn as a plaid or maud, and is the
same as Dandie Dinmont calls a grey marled
maud (and he appears seldom to have gone without one), they are now made in all the different
clan patterns.

The plaid, as worn in the Highland costume, is
fastened with a brooch on the left shoulder, and
is doubtless of very ancient origin. King Robert
the Bruce's brooch was presented by the Hon.
Fox Maule to Prince Albert, on the occasion of
her Majesty's visit to Scotland. The Low-
landers, on the contrary, use the right shoulder,
as in Sir Walter Scott's monument at Glasgow.

The Highland regiments wear the plaid in full dress: the 42d use the Campbell, the 71st the Mackenzie (or M'Leod), the 72d wear the Prince Charlie, the 74th have adopted the Forbes, the 78th a smaller set of Mackenzie, the 79th *what is called* the Cameron, or M'Donald, with yellow stripe, the 92d have the Gordon with the single stripe of yellow, and the 93d the large Campbell, generally called the Sutherland.

These are all worn open at the ends, and about 3½ yards in length, in fine woollen, or a coarser kind for undress, the silk poplin being much out of use since the woollen plaids are made in such fine material.

The maud, on the contrary, is generally shut or sewed up at one end. When worn by the shepherds and drovers, who often carry provisions and other articles of use in it—sometimes a young lamb!—it is called a 'pock,' or 'neuke;' and the old adage, to live on your ain ' pock neuke,' may come from this. But, as it has been observed before, for usefulness generally, and for covering a bed, those with both ends open and fringed are the best. When sewn up at one end no tie or brooch is required, as the left elbow is generally poked into it and acts as a purchase to wrap one's self tightly in it. [1]

I am credibly informed that the trade of this place (Galashiels) in 1830 could not be more, altogether, than £20,000; in Scotch goods *per se*, not more, certainly, than £2000. There were only about ten sets of machinery in the whole place; and, allowing for the kind of wool which was used at the time, could not turn out more than £2000 each set, which would make £20,000. But the introduction of Botany, Cape, and Australian wools, and more sets of machinery, now upwards of fifty sets, together with steam power, this amount you may now fairly multiply by 10, say £250,000. Its wealth now cannot be hid—her cold shielings are turned into comfortable domiciles—on her tables, where muslin kail was the fare, now is seen good roast beef; and, instead of hodden grey of their own making, they now much prefer good English broad cloth. I remember going to the Free

---

[1] It is observed in the paintings of Eastern Costume, by our townsman, Roberts, that the colours and manner of dress very much resemble the Scotch Highlander, especially the style of wearing their robe. May not Tartan have originated In Tartary?

Church in a suit of their best Tweeds, no doubt coarse enough looking, and of being taken to task by one of the ruling members, who said I was *daft*, and not very respectably *put on* for coming to the house of prayer. ' Coming events cast their shadows before;' and I have lived to see, as I prophesied it would be, nearly all the gentlemen who walk in Regent Street and the Parks clothed in the same stuff, and of a sound mind. Ye shades of shepherds,—who once trode her slopes and hill-sides, and who, no doubt, often sang in the adjacent dells, the beautiful airs of Galashiels, or Sour Plumbs, and Doun the Burn Davie,—cast your eyes now to her magistrates and Peel's police; her trades' dinners and inns, her doctors, her banks, and her fancy balls.

Minnow and partail fishing are so fully described by Stoddart and others, that I will only endeavour to give a few hints of my own, so as at once to bring it before you. As for the first of these, it is always a difficult matter to get them for the day that will suit you to fish with them; but if you can get them, and the water be dark coloured, there is no better bait; also, when the water is very low and clear (in fact, the two extremes), have a swivel and two hooks, one

tied a little above the other, and one bigger than
the other. Thus, with round bends.

Insert the large one in at the mouth, and bring
it out near the tail,—the small one through the
two lips or mouth of the minnow ; and in rapids
or tails of rough places, and where you would
not think a trout could lie for the strength of
the current, you will find them. Unless plenty
of water, do not cast twice in the same place;
as they generally hook themselves, especially in
rapid places. Where the river is broad, always
draw your bait to the side before you cast
again, and do it gently, or rather swing it out ;
but as you often lose your bait by its being
bitten at by large trout, for they are always the
biggest that take this bait or partail, I prefer
the last mentioned to the other. Partail, then, is
my favourite, being generally easiest got, and
stands throwing much longer. In my younger
days, no person could tell what a par was, not
even chemist and philosopher Davie, or the New

Chancellor.[1] It is now pretty well known to be the young of the salmon (a small trout or smolt does, for salmon, equally well). Stoddart has shown how to put this on, but I generally do it differently. I divide the tail, and cut up off the back, near the size of a good minnow, cutting off the back fin. An old and accomplished fisher, John Redhead, whose flies, both for salmon and trout, were the most successful I ever tried, taught me to sew the par and smolt's tail on the hook. He was a good scholar, and wrote in my book the following beautiful lines on the snow-drop in March :—

' Already now the snow drop dares appear,
The first pale blossom of the unripen'd year,
As if *Flora's* voice, by some transforming power
Had changed an icicle into a flower.
Its name and hue, the scentless plant retains,
And Winter lingers in its icy veins.'

The partail takes equally well, and stands much longer on the hook ; in fact, the more it is torn and bitten with trout, they seem to take the better ; and you can cast it farther than even worm or minnow, as you have well fixed it on

[1] Lord Brougham at Edinburgh.

your hook by a needle and whitey brown thread
out of your fly book. It is to be angled with,
in the same places as you would use the minnow, and in the same way, but, with this difference, it must be always kept spinning well in
the water, your tackle lightly leaded, and generally two swivels; as in sheep-washing time, I have
seen bits of wool interfere, and two I always
found best,—two hooks, one placed above the
other. But, where you have a strong and a
large stream, and you know there are big chaps
to be got, you may add a devil, as it is called,—
Three hooks back to back *beyond* the other two.
But this gear prevents its spinning in an ordinary
stream. Now, before you begin this most exciting of all trout fishing, put on a small fly hook,
and, in shallow places, catch, at least, three
smoults or par, and put them in a small case or
in your basket. There is little said against
this in the New Tweed Bill of 1859,—on other
rivers, I never saw it noticed by any body.
March and April are the best months for this
kind of fishing. When you get into May, you
can generally get the creeper and stone fly in
any of the tributaries of the Tweed, and on its
banks in thousands, where the river shelves

away to deeper water and leaves pretty large stones and shingle. In the Tweed and Don these are reckoned the best months for fly, and later in the season, when they do not rise to the fly so readily, the partail may then be resorted to.

In looking for creepers, get a small tin case like a snuff box, and go to a place of the river where there has been a continuous run of the river, and searching under the stones or gravel, you will soon see the creepers. Catch, then, say a dozen or two, if there be plenty, and put them into your box; use the same kind of hooks as you would do for minnow, only small *wee hookies* reversely tied, one above the other, insert one through the shoulder and the other at the tail. In clear water drop it above you, and fish up stream, casting rather diagonally, and letting the bait come down the stream; when opposite to you, cast again. It is very curious to observe, that, while the creeper and stone-fly,— for it follows the other in the course of nature,— while the one increases on the ferns the other decreases in the shingle; while they last *in* and *on* the water, few trout are to be had with the artificial fly. I have often heard the remark by

those who did not observe the signs of the times,
" how is it that we see so many fine trout rising
all around us, and not one of them will look at
our flies ?" They were busy at other 'Jaw wark,'
as the country man said to his landlord, when he
presented him with a present of nuts all ready
cracked and ready to eat. In fact, it is needless,
under these circumstances, to pursue your sport,
mayhap, till the evening. And now, I could wish
that the history of the stone or May fly had been
in better hands than mine. In the first place,
then, you will observe in eddies and other slow
running and shallow places, bits of stick or straw
sticking together and lying at the bottom. These
are generally the caddis worm, before it becomes
the creeper with a number of legs ; it then
creeps toward more stony places and gravel beds,
where, as the season advances, it gradually grows
larger. During the time this is going forward,
it is all the while changing and becoming the
stone or May fly, before it assumes its wings.
It has, during this time, gradually left the wet
places and got under the stones which lie nearly
dry, but, at the same time, quite close on the
edge of the river. About the end of May, if the
season is warm, or, more generally, the beginning

of June, it altogether leaves or creeps out of this
case or shell which has many feet, a large and
beautiful fly, having two pair of wings, the outer
large and the inner much smaller, which lie
close to its back, and not like those of the
ephemera fly, which stick cocked up. It keeps
under stones, but gradually, while the sun is out
or smiling, leaves them and settles on the trees
or brackens in its vicinity.[1] The female is the
largest, and comes into the world already prepared for supplying it again with the species, as
behind the wings and on her back she carries
her whole future brood, though not yet fecun-
dated by the male fly; but nature is kind in this
instance, and, as their time is short, like the wise,
they make the most of it, and soon draw together,
and she is very soon seen seemingly carrying
the male insect on her back, over the rough
places, both apparently very much delighted.
After this, like the common pigeon, they take
wing in air, in pairs, and unless in her short
flight she be snapped up by a large trout, the
female then drops the ova in the water,—these,
when seen through a magnifying glass, are

[1] This is not the green drake or dragon fly we see on
the Thames about Maidenhead.

beautifully formed little eggs of a blackish colour. Thus, is renewed the process of the caddis worm to the creeper, then to the stone or May fly, for next season. What a wonderful and beautiful process of nature do we behold here, every way deserving the study of the naturalist; life by gradual stages, going on and renewing itself, and creating and renewing food for the inhabiters of the streams. For, be it observed, that just in proportion as food is found, will we find fish in the rivers; and, according to the size of, or the volume of water which fills their bed, will fish, in a general way, be found small or great. When this fly, then, comes on the water, for the first two or three days you will almost always get large trout, and they much prefer the female fly to the male,—afterwards, the small fry getting knowing, begin to seize it also, and this I have found over and over again. I suppose trout of about ¼ lb. have not courage to seize so large a prey, or, perhaps, never before saw these lady queens on the water. The tackle for these flies is just like that for minnow, only made of trout fly hooks of the round bend and the smallest size, tied thus, on the finest gut and darkish coloured.

Insert one into the body and the upper one through the neck; and, as old Isaak says, of the frog, do this as if you loved it,—so as the hooks

may be undermost and the wings keep fluttering on the top of the water. And whoever says that you may fish with it sunk or under the water, I can only say from long experience, and from that of other noted May fly fishers, that I will eat all he catches, before dinner, and not ask a dram after them. Some use it most effectually, fishing only with an ordinary fly-hook, and with the wings cut off; but you must strike quickly on the rise of the trout; endeavour to get the wind on your back, and fish up the stream in all cases, as it will only do in clear water and sunshine, at least, that is its best time. Rather jerk it forward, and do not fish with a line longer than your rod; and if you have a light stiff rod of eleven or twelve feet, use it in preference to any other; throw diagonally up and let the fly come down opposite to you, then cast again. Miss any ripple or swirl near a stone, if you do not want to engage a big fellow, as there they always lie watching their prey; for trouts, unlike the arch enemy, do not roam up and down at this time. But you must cast to all holes and corners, with a clear conscience and a quick eye, to the filling of your pannier by honest fishing Be aye ready to land your fish, and, therefore, keep near the side and cast toward the middle, this will enable you to do so, easily, for, in Scotch rivers, we seldom carry a landing-net. But, if you can wade up the middle of the stream, and make your cast from side to side, like a clock pendulum, then do it. Now, suppose you have caught a dozen or two of these flies, no easy matter, for they run very swiftly and hide in a twinkling below the stones, they also have a most extraordinary facility of dropping themselves off the brackens and disappearing in the grass; you must be prepared with a box, the same as you have for the creepers ; but a little experience will soon show you that this, like Touchstone's 'mustard, is naught.' You must, then, be prepared with a tin case, made like unto an horn, with a lid at the small end of it ; and when you need to replenish your hook,—which is at times very often,—you can take out one without losing the whole *bink*. Now,

by far the best way is to get a good sized cow-
horn prepared, and having bunged up the larger
end, and made a small hole at the other, large
enough to admit your forefinger, fit a cork and
attach it to the end, with a bit of string; having
previously perforated the horn with holes, the
size that a good oaten straw might enter (the one
now before me, made I believe, fifty years ago,
for the Eden, has the testamental number of
seventy and seven in it); through other two holes
put a piece of cord, in length so as to hang it
round your neck, the whole will be complete and
useful for your purposes. To those who fish
much,—and I have known some who do so
nearly the whole year, as you shall hear,—the
May fly comes as a new thing, in its way, and
as it lasts only a fortnight or three weeks, I like
to keep to it while I have it, and, therefore,
recommend it as a capital relief to those who
fish much during the early months with other
baits. I remember being in the Highlands
on a fishing excursion, and living in the
same inn with a gentleman, a very great
enthusiast in Ichthyology and the sport;
when sitting over our toddy,—after a capital
day's work in sea-trouts,—along with my friend

Mill, who accompanied me,—that a long confab on the subject was most absurdly brought to an end by the following turn in the conversation :—

Piscator. It appears then, sir, that you spend a great deal of your time in fishing?

Gent. Yes I do, friend, from eight to nine months in the year.

Pis. Of one who is so devoted to the sport, may I be permitted to ask, how you spend the other three or four months?

Gent. Ha', Sir, I hie me home and betake myself to my books, etc.

Mill. But, could you not fill up the other three or four months with your favourite sport also?

Gent. (Excited), Ha', my dear friend, tell me, ha' tell, where I could do so?

Mill. At the Bullers o' Buchan, for skate.

Before I pass on to the Tweed and Don, I must notice the Ettrick, but I never fished it above Selkirk,—for who would do so, unless assured of fine conditioned water, when he has all the fine casts of the Tweed in the neigh-bourhood, which will be noticed in due time. There are good trout in this river, however; but I am afraid that the mills are destroying them below the town, for with sorrow did I see there, the other day, the commencement of a tannerie quite close to the mill-lead, and there are no tanks used.

Selkirk

Stands on the south side of the Ettrick, on the face of a hill, 'The Birse,' and the Sutors of Selkirk are well known. It is famous, inasmuch as they can show the colours which they brought off from the fatal battle of Flodden Field in 1513, and which I have seen. Its men, 'The Flowers of the Forest,' being, it is said, the only body who kept the field and were in battle array next morning after the ever to be lamented event. It is now a thriving place, the mills of Roberts, Brown, and Waddle, giving employment to many hands. The *lap-stone* has thus given place to the *shuttle.* I may mention an instance of generosity here. In the time of scarcity of water, Lord Napier allows the mill-owners to draw freely on the Loch of St Mary; this is regulated by means of a sluice near the loch; no doubt, in 1859, so dry a season, the fish would get a fright, as many feet of water from

the surface was drawn off to turn the wheels.
There is a little good fishing water below the
bridge, near its confluence with the Tweed,
also above the bridge at Selkirk, and, when the
water is big, you will see, in defiance of all law,
and in open day light, poachers picking off the
sea-trout and salmon in great numbers, as they
run up the dam-dike or cauld, to spawn. In
close time I have seen two or three taken in as
many minutes while I passed by, the villanous
rascals having no thought but how to kill 'twa
at a blow,' if they could. It is a fine pastoral
walk from this place to St Mary's Loch ; the
distance, about sixteen miles, you can rest and
be thankful at Tibby Shiels (now Mrs Richard-
son), and you will, no doubt, find yourself comfortable there, and feel yourselves, like old Isaak
and his friends, in clean beds with sheets smell-
ing sweet of lavender. You can then return to the
Tweed *via* Traquair to Inverleithen or Peebles.
To those who would desire a solitary walk for
contemplation, or opportunity for a long quiet
gossip by themselves, which, in the midst of this
busy world, is not often found, when they
wish to return to Edinburgh, let them take such
a horse as Bishop Jewel presented to Richard

Hooker, viz., a good walking stick, and go forth by the road now made by Inverleithen kirk up the Leithen Water between hills, until they get near Middleton Muir. The distance is nearly seventeen miles. I once took this road and thought it would never have an end.

> ' Gif way to heaven be sic a road,
> I'll sit me down and weary.'
>
> *Old song.*

At Roxburgh, the remains of the castle are only seen. Here it was that James II. of Scotland was killed in 1460, by the bursting of a cannon, made probably from the trunk of a tree, and hooped all round with iron.

Kelso.

Kelso is situated on the Tweed, in the very heart of fishing ground, near its confluence with the Teviot, a capital trouting river. It has a very fine ruin of a monastery, and a beautiful bridge over the Tweed. The Duke of Roxburghe's seat, Floors, is to the westward of the town, which is not a manufacturing place like Hawick or Galashiels, being situated in a purely agricultural district. The proper flies for both

rivers can be purchased at Mr Forrest's, and
James Wright, Sprouston, is a capital maker of
both salmon and trout flies. If you stop a day
or two, or even ten days, at this place, you should
devote the most of your time to the Teviot,[1]
beginning at the Tweed Bridge and up to Roxburgh Station, and beyond it up and down, but,
remember that you cannot fish it well unless
you wade, as the river flows into deep places,
over a shelving rocky bed, and you must not
heed wetting your feet if you are desirous to fill
your basket. It is a first rate river for trout ;
and, if you have the water in order, you will no
doubt, be rewarded. But, keep in mind, that in
this recreation as well as in all the various busi-
nesses of life's bustle, you will find that

> ' According as your labours rise,
> So your rewards increase.'

And I remember detecting a friend of mine
killing a salmon with a big stone, and quietly
humming to the tune of ' A' the Airts the Wind
can Blaw,' the concluding line of the verse,

> ' And all her paths are peace.'

[1] There was a good place for shelter, or ham and egg
near a Mrs Hogg's.

They say that you are now challenged if you fish here, but I never was, and whenever I go again, I hope to be used in the same way, especially as I fish only for trout and for sport, and not for the pot.

The Tweed is very wide and beautiful here, having, by this time, swallowed up so many of its tributaries, and I cannot do better to the memory of my dear friend Alexander Hume (who, a few years ago, published two small volumes of Scottish Songs, etc., well worth reading), than here quote from his song of the Tweed. I like it much, and it is little known. The Tweed has its origin 1500 feet above the level of the sea, in a hill of Peeblesshire. The same hill sends forth the rivers Clyde and Annan.

Song of Tweed.

' O bonnie Tweed, rin on, and may you ever rin
    as clear
As ye do now in loveliness, for mony a coming year ;
May ilka bonnie flower that blooms, may ilka
    blooming weed
That looks on you, plead to the sun for blessings
    on ye Tweed.'

Leaving Kelso and going up the river, you

have not only beautiful scenery but good fishing, and it rejoiceth me to say, that you may fish
the whole river, from Berwick to Tweedsmuir,
for trout, without being challenged by any one.
The salmon alone are the protected denizens of
the river, each salmon fishing being rented at
high rates, and each having its keeper. The
right to the salmon, by late decisions of the
Sheriff, not giving the exclusive right to trout
also. Long may this privilege continue for the
recreation, the health, and the enjoyment of
those in towns and cities pent, and those also who
dwell on Tweed's bonnie banks! The trout are
large here, and you may sometimes take two and
three pounders. If you kill a grilse, it must be
given up, or you can buy it at the market price,
from the taxsman. If the day be fine, you may
be sure to fill your basket before you get to St
Boswell's Green, where you can either stay or
get on to Melrose. It would be absurd to say
much of a place so well known and so often described. I shall never forget, while visiting this
beautiful old ruin, my friend Mill's recitation of
" those Evening Bells " in the Church-yard—it
had just struck seven. There is good fishing water
to this, and up to Abbotsford, and, if time is not

pressing, it will, no doubt, repay your labour. You must now take to a double-handed rod, if you have one, for the water is strong and wide, adapting, of course, any kind of bait you think may suit. As a general rule, when I have seen the fly persevered in the whole of the day, reckoning at the end of it, it has, on most occasions, *come far ben*. In fact, I have found it, in most instances, the most successful, provided you get over a good deal of water,—say five or six miles a day. In ordinary fishing, you should never go less than two or three miles an hour ; for, if you can only occasionally hie to the river side for health and recreation, it is amazing how much you can get over, being fresh men and fresh minded. How soon now do you get to your destinations, per rail, not as it used to be, —say to Kelso, by Soutra Hill—coachman and guard, and a ride of four hours or so, and perhaps in the rain all the way. What a social world the men who are in it should make it, by the unheard of speed we now can visit places, and our friends ! What a splendid tribute to the genius of Stephenson and Brunel, is thus paid ! That we can attend the sick-bed of a dying mother or father, and bid farewell, hand in hand, to those of our friends who are departing from our shores, perhaps alas! for ever. What is this earth, and all it gives us, unless we cultivate, and have friendships, without which, as Shakespear says, we become 'Blocks and stones, and worse than senseless things;' and Sterne says, 'He would go fifty miles a-foot to kiss the hand of the man who pretended not to criticise his author.' By the same rule, he would now go five hundred. Thus do our senses change our ideas, and they, in their turn, lead us up to higher ones still, 'Till to perfection we arrive.'

I remember, a few years ago, leaving London by the Great Northern at nine P.M., and being at Berwick-on-Tweed by a little after six A.M., quite wonderful; and getting to '*our cottage*' at Thornilee, I rested the Sabbath-day, far away from the busy haunts of men, and literally without an address, for no one knew of my whereabouts. Here I was far beyond the post-man's knock,—my address known only to my-self. I remember a Cockney friend of mine graphically giving me an account of his feel-ings at being without an address. He had been wandering among the Highlands of Scot-

land for some weeks, and had not written home
nor heard from thence, and found himself
curiously situated and quite alone on some step-
ping-stones which led a considerable way into
a loch somewhere betwixt Loch Lomond and
Loch Tay. It all at once occurred to him that
he stood, as it were, alone in the midst of the
world. On casting his eyes around, it so hap-
pened as if every moving and creeping thing
on the face of the earth had hid itself. No
lambkins sported near, nor shepherds piped on
the lea. The descending sun was casting its
long streaks of light and shade on the scene,
shadowing the sides of the mighty hills, deep
and motionless, into the waters of the lake, in a
way which all the 'caulk and keel' of Salvator
Rosa or Claude can give but a faint idea of.
As he looked around on this calm and pleasing
prospect, he was struck with the grandeur of
the panorama. The mountains near and at a
distance seemed, by their profound stillness, to
be awaiting some awful event that was about to
befall. Yet he thought of 'home and beauty,'
—he thought of Bond Street, he thought of
scales, weights, and measures,—of the many
pounds of tea and coffee that had been served

out that morning to the many unwashed house-maids from the streets adjacent to his establishment. As to his young men, they knew nothing about him save that his name stood as bright in the gold letters above his door as ever, and that his shop was kept as regularly open from morn till night as before. He also imagined that as many carriages and people would be passing his windows as when he stood at the door of his house. But now, where was he!—On the bounds of eternity! 'Awful thought!' said he to himself; 'were I to jump a yard or perhaps stir a foot, I might never again be heard of, my *address* being known only to myself; and having no relations, my goods and chattels, what would become of them in all the world!'

Sunday on Tweed Side.

Blessed be the Sabbath-day,—that day of quiet and delightful rest to all those who have exercised their minds during the week, on the amazing love of God towards them, and who have left busy cities for a time, and found themselves strangers

in the country. An indescribable calmness ushers
in the first day of the week. If we look up to
the hills at early morn, we may observe that
already in the very steps of the neighbouring
shepherd up their sides, there is something
which denotes a more sober and peaceful stride
than he had yesterday. If we listen, we hear
not, as at other times, the busy flail going in the
adjacent barn,—we see fewer travellers,—no
horsemen or carriages, save, perhaps, a solitary
gig carrying a family to church. To our piscatory friends in the South,—say at Richmond or
Maidenhead, this is the great day of all the week
for their sport of angling! but here we have no
such custom; and, I will venture to inform them,
that from Tweedsmuir to Tweedmouth, not a
line for salmon, salar, trout, or par, is cast on its
waters, so well is the Sunday kept on Tweed-
side!! But it may be said by some of our
Southern brethren of the angle, What are you
to do when in the country, on this day, if you
do not fish,—read? No, not entirely so. He
is a fisher seldom to be courted, who has not
added to his art some other acquirement besides
reading,—say botany, geology, entomology, or
sketching. In fact, we should reckon that man to

be but a poor flailer of a salmon stream, who did not ingraft on the *gentle art* a knowledge and love of one or the other of these beautiful studies (ever mindful to look through them up to God). On a lovely Sunday in the month of July, my friend of St John's and I finding ourselves alone together at our quarters on Tweed's beauteous banks, and at a very pastoral part of the river, issued forth to a charming spot where a baronial castle stands on the south side of the stream, faced on the opposite side by the remains of what is said to have been another of those ancient fastnesses,—the river running between them. Here also it divides itself, and forms a small island,—the south side a fine salmon run,—the other a good trout one. The hills on either side rise to a considerable height, and are, on looking upward, surmounted or crested by others still higher, the uncultivated angles of which breathe forth nothing that is exciting, but, on the contrary, a very pleasing repose,—

‘ The river rushing o'er its pebbled bed,
Imposes silence with a stilly sound.’

Here, on a bank of wild thyme and heather,

we sat ourselves down to study and to admire, while the sun shone forth beautifully, and oxlip, daisy and ladysmocks grew around us. To a healthy mind, what a delightful study would be the wild flowers of Ettrick Forest. 'The works of the Lord are great, sought out of all them that have pleasure therein.' With the help of a good pocket glass we were able to view most of the various and minute beauties of those 'that toil not neither do they spin.' First, then, near a marshy place, we pick up the mouse-eared hawkweed, or hilracium pilosella,—yellow and tinged with a purple hue outside of its petals,— then, its hairy covered stem, at the end of every particular hair of which we can discover a little globe of matter oozing out a yellow balm for the bees, which are all very busy in their way around us. The selfheal or prunella vulgaris, by the glass it appears a little bush of rhododendron, which we often love to admire fast by the waters of the busy Serpentine; but, to tell of the beauties of the yellow rattle or rhinanthus crista galli,—lotus, crow berry, cross wort, forget-me-not, all which were found in this place, with many others and many kinds of grasses, with

' Butter cups and daises,
And all the pretty flowers,'

would greatly exceed our designed limits, and
be far beyond our powers of description. On
returning to our cottage, we applied the micro-
scope to some of the very dust of their stems,
and beheld a new world opened to our eyes.
We walk the fields, yet how few of us consider
that we are often treading down so many
beautiful wild flowers, said to be the special gift
of the angels to our world.

Thus far have we endeavoured to give a short
sketch of the way in which we spend our Sunday at Thornilee, being seven miles from any
church. When thrown on our resources, it is
good to add something to our great fishing
propensities, for we oftentimes, while following
this pleasing occupation, hear ourselves say,
if we had but spent half of our valuable time
in the study of *The Book* which we have given
to fishing, it might have been better for us
to-day; however, we hope, even in this, that
we are filling up some useful segment in the
wide circle of life, which the great Fisher of
Men, when He comes to judge the earth, will
not disapprove.

In July especially, after some good floods, we have often good sport with the grilses or young salmon ; and the fly is the only lure I ever used to them. I have known them take May fly, and also minnows, at this time ; but fly is the readiest, and they are far more greedy on it now than when the season is farther advanced. It is also the most delightful time of the year to wade in, the water being of a mild temperature. But the real time of salmon fishing on Tweed (I speak of, perhaps forty miles up from the sea), is reckoned after the nets were taken off, which used to be 15th October, and we had to the 7th November inclusive, allowed for rod fishing only. This is now altered, and extended to the 30th November for the rod, and no other lure than fly allowed. I may mention, that the Bill of 1858, by some mismanagement, the Marquis of Westminster chairman of com-mittee, not clearly understanding the point, closed the nets on the 1st, and the rod fishing on the 14th October, and in allusion to this cir-cumstance, and the great many poachers who come from the adjacent towns at this time, the following appeared in the 'Border Advertiser' of Galashiels :—

ON THE CLOSING DAY OF SALMON FISHING ON TWEED, 1858.[1]

TUNE.—*Tibbie Fuller.*

Bonnie Tweed at Thornilee,
There's ower mony fishing at her;
Frae Berwick Brig to Stobo Kirk
Her banks are in a perfect hatter.
    Whipping at her, switching at her,
    Thrashing at her, leathering at her,
    Bonnie Tweed at Thornilee,
    There's ower mony fishing at her.

Six cam creeping o'er the hill,
Wabsters ten frae Gala Water;
Twa at Betty's, three at Tam's,
There name is Legion fishing at her.
    Whipping at her, etc.

Gif par or smoult but tak a midge,
They think they see *him* gee a splatter;
Syne twenty wands wave o'er its head,
W'i flees and worms and roen batter.
    Whipping at her, etc.
Gif a' their rods were laid at ends,
And a' their lines baith white and sable:

---

[1] The House of Lords having altered the day, 7th November, to 14th October.

The tain would be a guid Scotch mile,
The other length o' Atlantic's cable.
　　Whipping at her, etc.

Their *take* o' fish scarce thirty pounds
Avoirdupois, frae west and easter ;
I'd hang the loon who changed the law,
They ca' his name, I think, W—tm—er.
　　Whipping at her, switching at her,
　　Thrashing at her, leathering at her ;[1]
　　Bonnie Tweed at Thornilee,
　　There's ower mony fishing at her.

　　　　　　　　　　　J. L.

Now, in former times, early in the season,
when the river opened, say 1st March, a large
fly very gaudy, or worm, was used, and I have
seen good sport with partail and minnow. I
remember being at the Caddon Foot Pool, and
of going most carefully over it with the fly, viz.,
Tom Purday and the *butcher*, without seeing a
fin. A few minutes afterwards, a Galashiels
weaver essayed the same with partail, and, at
the very first cast, hooked a salmon of 16 lbs,
which I killed for him, he nearly losing it with

---

[1] A celebrated fisher at Peel, whose constant applica-
tion at the water earned for himself the *soubriquet* of
Lord *Leatherawa*.

foolish endeavours to catch it by the tail. About September and October, and when the mornings are frosty and clear, the most deadly kind of fishing is perhaps with the worm, either on smooth bottoms thrown toward the deep side, or, casting it like a fly, on the most rapid places; this may be done either by baiting one large hook with two large worms, or having two or even three large hooks, all hanging nearly in a bunch, two worms on each hook,—they like a good mouthful,—and so much for the often repeated idea, that salmon *eat nothing.* No doubt, I never found any thing in the stomach of a salmon ; he is a healthy fish, and of a very quick digestion. I once was eye witness to this fact, having seen five or six taken one morning before breakfast, from a pool near Ashiestiel, in this same way. While this may be good sport to those who like it, I never exercise it; the filthy bag full of moss and our last enemy I cannot abide, and the difficulty of obtaining them also is another objection. I have seen two or three of us go out at darkening to the garden, with spade and grape, and flaming tallow candles, and a scene worthy of Rembrandt, ensued. I have already said you should, in fishing, get over your ground at the rate of two miles an hour. In fishing for salmon,[1] however, it is generally in the different pools, and you warm yourself while you make your way to the next one you intend to fish, it may be a mile up or perhaps a mile down, the river. This, no doubt, sounds strange to our Cockney friends, who, accustomed to fish in position, in patience, and in a punt, know little about the capturing of salmo salar; for, instead of sitting at your ease, with bottled stout, pipes and tobacco, you walk along the banks, —around you the calm and peaceful hills, with the Baronial Castle in the distance ; the flowing and winding river ; the shaking of the trees of the valley, the oak, the beech, and the fir; the gentle breeze, 'the incense breathing morn,' curling the surface of the pools ; the singing of the water crow,[2] in its notes not unlike the canary—the only bird which at present puts forth its song, save the robin's plaintive notes, at this season, ' fa' o' the leaf.' But, hark, you

[1] Salmon are not found across the line ; although, I have been credibly informed by a friend, there are trout streams in New Zealand.

[2] I seldom or ever saw this bird on the Don; formerly there was a reward given for shooting him on Tweed.

hear a heavy wafting of the air above you, it is
the heron away before you to some sequestered
cairn. He loves solitude, as a bird of the desert,
and all alone, steps into the shallow places after
his prey. Look! he stands to consider a while,
but he hears our approach, and, as he cares not
for busy men, and would rather not hear their
tattle, he mounts again on the wing into mid
air, and away to some other lonely dell. He
prefers to pursue his way unobserved and un-
seen. He seeks his bread in the *living* waters,
which he swallows with gladness. Thus he is to
us a pattern of meekness, while he will not let a
stranger intermeddle with his joy. But I
have now arrived at the bit where a fish, if any
should show himself, for well do those who fish
often know the *lairs*. He rose, but not hooked ;
we cast again, but no answer. I would recommend all, if ever in the same predicament, to
recede a few yards and wait for seven or eight
minutes. I cast again, he shows himself, and
immediately feel the weight of 18 lbs. Dutch at
the end of the line. A little excited not to lose
this, as two others were lost during the morning,
I give him a little at first of his own way, seeing
that he keeps the middle of the stream, and seems

to covet concealment. I lay a cautious pressure on my tackle, and turn his head down the water. Now comes the tug of war, to the tune of salmon tails up the water. He was wild. He leapt up. He sprung in air. The bir and whir of my reel admonished me to keep my fingers out of the lines' way, for I felt as if something was applying a hot wire to them.

> A bir a whir, a salmon's on,
> A glorious fish, a thumper ;
> And if we land him, we shall have
> Another glorious bumper.

At times somersetting like a very Ducrow, at others like an arrow from the bow of Jonathan, which returned not empty, jumping up and most cunningly endeavouring to twist his tail over the line, which, of course, was kept perpendicular as the York column,—rod all the while at half a circle, down the stream he went, drawing all with him, 'like Beauty with a single hair.' After slipping my feet, and grazing the skin off my shins, and nearly breaking my arm, on recovering myself, I found that he still stuck to the end of my line,—but there were ' envious osiers' a-head. I made a stand, and, after a hard battle of thirty-five to fifty minutes, I got a clean fish of 19 lbs., and found my fore finger cut to the bone with the run of the line.

There are times, while fishing, either for salmon or trout, in which you will observe, that although there are plenty of fish in the river, you strive in vain, by changes of fly, to take them. They will even come up and flap the fly with their tail, and keep floundering about you in all directions. This is a sure sign of a change of weather or of a flood coming. From long observation, there is not, I may say, a better weather glass; and, if you are wise, you will give it up and betake yourselves to your books or something else; for the wielding of a rod, some eighteen-and-a-half feet long all day, is no joke. If they take that day at all, it will just be when the sun dips below the horizon. I have seen a pool fished over and over again, without success; but a knowing one behind, on the bank looking on, watched our leaving it, and before we had got a quarter of a mile nearer to our dinner, we could see, making a movement like old Lot's wife, by the bend of the rod and the steady walk by the margin of the pool, true indications of a good fish being already on the line.

The true salmon fisher is generally said to fish with only one fly. For myself I *confess* the bob. With two flies you need not make so great an angle as is generally done,—that is to say, you may cast straighter across the stream ; for, it often happens, your trail fly may not be sufficiently cast out, and your bob falling over the fish, he immediately takes it, where, had it only been the bend of your line, it would but have scared him. I remember once having hooked a fish with the trail fly, and, as I worked him up and down the pool, the bob fly dangling about half a yard above the water, another took it. 'The pleasantest angling is to see the fish cut, with her golden oars, the silver stream, and greedily devour the treacherous bait.'[1] The rise at it was very beautiful; with the sudden jerk of the line, I lost the other. They were lovely, but I am sorry to add, that in their deaths, they were divided,—since the one, no doubt, went up to Peebles, while the other went into my bag, so you see I did not lose any thing by having a *bobber*. It is a much disputed point, however, much insisted on by Lord Lovat, I believe. Another day, near the end of the season,

[1] Much ado about nothing, Act iii. scene 1.

the shepherd of a neighbouring farm hooked a
fish, which, while he ran, another fish followed it
all over the pool, that could he have used his gaff
while holding the rod, he, might have killed
both, so close did it follow the other to the
side. Spawning season can only account for this
piscatory fact. Much has been said about striking your fish. This may be done when fishing
for trout ; but, so far as I have found and experienced,—never for salmon. Many a good line
have I seen broken by this process. When the
water is heavy, and when you may fish with
double gut, even to the fly, then you may do as
you like ; but if you are fishing with three or
four links of single gut, and the water clear and
not very deep, let the fish, I say, hook themselves.
If you *harle* so as to keep the fly on or near the
top of the water whenever you see a fish rise,
if he has taken the hook you have only to
raise the point of the rod, and he is generally
quite secure,—some again sink their fly so low
in the water, that the beauty of the rise is never
seen (but which I dearly love to behold), and a
deadly way it is, for the heaviest fish often take
it then. Still, I would recommend only to raise
the point of your rod.

𝔅urning the 𝔚ater.

But our sport is often spoiled through the day
(on Tweed), by poachers through the night
especially. If the water is low, we are often
awakened from our peaceful slumbers by noises
and the glare of lights. On looking out we
soon see the cause,—*the spunkies* are out burning the water, as it is called. This process consists of six or seven men or callants, one carrying
the light or iron lantern, fixed to the end of a
pole, some six feet in length, filled either with
parrot coal, fir wood, or any combustible stuff
which can make a flaming light on the water.
On approaching redds or shallow places, or
spawning beds, and especially streams, where,
with the glare of the light, the fish, to an experienced eye, are easily seen (for my part, I
might gaze until I was black and blue in the
face, or ere I could distinguish one from a
stone), another of the party aye ready with a
'three tae'd leister on his shouther,' at the end
of some long sapling ash, which has been lately

sacrificed to their wants, from nine to twelve feet in length, darts this weapon at the fish,

> 'The shaft glides swiftly through his horny hands,
> And quick as lightning o'er the fish he stands,'

springing at the same time into the water, sometimes up to his middle, pinning the fish to the bottom as it were, and, which is immediately secured and thrown out to the standers by, at the side. This, of course, is illicit or *black* fishing. I have seen three or four burnings all going on the same night,—and all the laws that are made, and all the watchers that are put on, cannot stop this. As an instance of destructiveness in this way, a poacher of Selkirk, well known to be so, when asked by a friend, in a quiet way, how many were killed in a week? answered *dryly*, he did not know how many others took, but for his part, along with two others of the same profession, he took off the Howden Rack below Yair Bridge, during one night, four corn sacks full. I have been told by an old man, and a keen fisher too, that long ago, when there were few or no restrictions on fresh water or other fish, nothing of night or net fishing was heard of, but that whenever gentlemen began to preserve their different waters, and hounded off any one who dared approach them, all kinds of gins and *hair* nets, for their capture, came into use. A real fisher, for the love of the thing, is just as scarce as the real poet; but if you set man-traps and spring guns, and issue laws against it, the effect will be to make many men fish who never otherwise would have done so, just out of contradiction, and from a certain excitement which this very thing produces. If the waters were all open, in my opinion, there would be fewer fishers; and if there were more inclined to it, the fish would still be as plentiful, and, doubtless, more so, as each true angler would be partly and individually interested in their preservation. The Tweed, as I have said, being free to trout fishers, it may be a question, whether this is not really in the favour of its being a salmon river, as we all know, large trout devour a great deal of the spawn and the small fry,—small did I say,—I have often killed them just gorged with par and smolts often three and four inches long. In this state they are often very fond of taking the fly, probably by way of *dram.* Sometimes in going out to the river, although you may have seen fish the evening before, rising in the different pools, you fish in vain. They have come up together by a flood, and have passed your quarters, in fact, they are generally *working*, while the river continues pretty large, up to the higher spawning beds, and you experience what we sometimes call a *vacancy*, or the fish have not yet settled in the pools, and if you continue to fish, you may have sport, by casting on the most unlikely places and in thin water. I remember one November afternoon, toward the close of the day, I went out to try the Howgate, and pulling on a large fly (for I prefer such, with a good deal of the golden pheasants feathers for evening), at the second or third cast I had *him* fast, and felt him pretty heavy, he went off nobly down the stream, and out went the line in a whir. He then made a rush up to the old spot, with a most determined perseverance, tried to break me; but the bold Robin Hood of the waters had met with his match, and we fought hard a long time. I heard footsteps passing along, and I called up the bank to the road, but it now being dark below, although the sky was clear above, I only alarmed *twa gouks*, passing by, who declared that they could neither see me nor the fish, which I said I had on my line;

having fallen down, and only recovering myself by the assistance of one of them, who endeavoured to gaff him, but in vain. As I had only on single gut, I could use little freedom with him. He did, however, strike him ; and away he went again, in the dark, with the broken gaff sticking in his back, and marking his whereabouts in the water ; and, after a run of nearly two hours, I had the satisfaction of killing a fish, a strong red kipper of 18 or 19 lbs., under the sweet influences of Orion and the Pleiades. On taking up my rod it felt like a toy in my hands, and my arms were much inclined to rise toward my head all the rest of the evening. I was told, on my return, that the neighbouring shepherd had hooked a large fish in the morning, had run him in all the various ways, and that, worn out and quite done for with the exertion, having swam across the river twice,—rather heavy at the time, —with his rod in his teeth, he had gone home about three o'clock in the afternoon, to enjoy the poppies of Morpheus. Ye Richmond and Teddington fishers, call ye that patience!! While I now sit and write this, I see on the opposite side of the river, three or four poachers with leister and rake hooks, 'casting their glamour

ower them.' See, they have drawn a large one
out of the stream, with the rake hooks, while one
below is killing another; this is in the fair light
of day, and in defiance of all law and Tweed
Acts. October and November are, no doubt, the
most uncertain season for fishing salmon, on account of frost and wind, accompanied with fallen leaves; it was seldom that in the three weeks
from the close of the nets, we ever got what
might be called a good day's sport at this
time of the year.

I will only conclude this short and imperfect
sketch of doings on the Tweed, by quoting a
few words from the letter of a friend whom
I requested to write me, as I left it at the close
of 1848:—'From the day you left to the end of
the rod fishing, 7th November, there were no fish
taken in this quarter but by the spear or burning
the water; I am sorry to say it was about as
poor a finish as mortal man could conceive.'

For these twenty years and more the fishing
in the upper waters of Tweed has been falling
off ; and I would caution any angler, in coming
so far up, from expecting anything like sport.
It is too far from the sea,—the fish are not in
season, and, for the most part, blackish at this

time, and seldom rise to the fly greedily. I have seen a fish rise to the fly, and though often changed on him, say five or six times, yet never take it to HIS LIPS. Need we wonder, then, at the rake and leister modes of taking him in the 'back end.' In fact, in the vicinity of manufacturing places and tanneries, where lime is used,[1] I am afraid all fishing will soon be put an end to. What with sending down all kinds of dying matters,—such is the filth below Galashiels, for instance,—and the common sewers of every town on the banks, going on increasing, [see what has been already said on this subject at page 8.], anything like good fishing will shortly not be had, unless far away in the North, and it is now not an uncommon thing to see gentlemen who go to Norway and even Iceland for their favourite sport of salmon fishing. The Tweed, where I now am, runs smaller than it did twenty-five years ago. Drainage, of course, is mainly the cause of this; it also gets lower in the

---

[1] The destructiveness of lime is very great. When the new bridge of Ashiestiel was first begun, a great part of it fell, and such was the destruction of fish in consequence of the lime, that the country folks gathered the fish up at the sides of the river in TUB-FULLS.

summer time than formerly,—the very natural consequence of this improvement. In great and continued rains it comes down and fills its wonted banks, from brae to brae; but it soon runs off, excepting in the winter months. This, I am afraid, is the real cause of the falling off of fish in the river; for, I suppose, few districts were ever more improved during the last thirty years than these of Gala and Tweed. The farmers are now up and doing. I remember, in a speech of Sir Robert Peel, I think, while introducing the Corn Laws in 1846, he said, so far as he had information, the land could be made to yield one third more than it then did. Guano and drainage have done much to fulfil this idea; but the manufacturing interests are clapping spurs to the sides of the agriculturists, and they will, in the end, have all the land in their own hands. As the House of *Commons* obtains more of this element, the entails of land, no doubt, will soon be broken up. Look at the lands I now behold opposite, in Ettrick. Can there be much improvement in nine years' leases ?—I say that it is a national loss to have estates so managed. We see now-a-days a great race running between landlordism and merchandise; and, in my opinion,

it is easy to see who will gain it.[1] But there was
much less fishing long ago than there is now, in
all of our rivers. No doubt, if the Tweed is to
continue a river, yielding fruit, it must be protected on its banks and also in its beds,—on its
banks from the destructive poacher, and in its
beds—from every filth that is now run into it by
the manufacturer. *This* is, no doubt, provided
for in the last Acts ; but the Commissioners, so
far as I can see, have let the rent of fishings drop
so low, that they cannot afford to put a sufficient
staff to stop the former, nor employ surveyors to
detect the others. If all such matter could be
saved—and I never could see much difficulty
in doing so—what is now sent into the rivers to
taint the streams for fish, cattle, and man, might
be made the great source of profit to the land, by
the system of tanks—look what can be done with
liquid manure. But I must now turn from the
Lowlands to the Highlands, and give you some
of my doings in Aberdeenshire.

[1] See the correspondence of Mr Irvine of Hawick, and
the Duke of Buccleuch, in the *Scotsman* of January 9,
1860. Next to keeping unpolluted streams for the drink
of man and beast, this is a most important subject for
the community.

Aberdeenshire.

BERDEEN is much improved since I first knew it, and there are few streets anywhere finer than Union Street—which, in its whole extent, is of white granite—and is really imposing. The city used to swarm with ragged children; but, I am happy to say, that the Ragged Schools, under the care and inspection of Sheriff Watson, have had a wonderful effect, and now you see scarcely one—in fact none—but all are attending schools of some kind during the day. This is a move in the right direction. There is a good statue of the Duke of Gordon, the 'Cock of the North,' as he was called, in the market place, and also two Russian guns, from the Crimea, which were lately presented to the town by Lord Panmure.[1]

---

[1] A most comical incident occurred with these shortly after they were placed here. A London sharper, observing a Highland clown gazing round them, quietly observed, that he was exposing them there for sale, and that he would take thirty shillings for the pair,—they to be

I shall begin with the first river in this county that I fished in, viz. :—

The Don.

The Don has its source about five miles above Corgarff. Its tributaries are the Bucket, Esset, and Ury, fed by burns Colpie, Kellock, Shevock, and Gady. It is nearly a quarter of a century since I first cast a fly on its streams. At that time the usual way of getting from London to its banks was per steamer, or by smack ; and many happy and pleasant days have I spent in the voyage. It is fished much in the same way as Tweed ; but, seven or eight miles from Aberdeen, you have a large volume of water, and the banks are not so shelving as the Tweed from Melrose to Peebles. Generally your flies are of a large kind ; and nearly all the salmon flies here, as well as on the Spey, are made of the heron hackle. This, no doubt, makes the fly *lively* in the water, and, generally, of a large kind, the

removed in the morning. The money was actually paid ; but when he came at the matin bell, with his horse and cart to take them away, the laughter and his dismay, may be well conceived, for it cannot be described.

pools being much deeper and darker; the Don
for most part coming through a great deal of
muir lands, and a good many peat moss burns
running into it in its course to the sea, which it
falls into a little to the north of the city of Aberdeen. The rivers here are all more or less protected, both for salmon and for trout. This, in a
measure, arises from large tracts of land belong-
ing to one proprietor, and on both sides of the
river, and not, as on the Tweed, which is divided
into so many small properties. You cannot cast
a fly for your amusement, at small fry in Don,
without being instantly challenged by some *gilly*
or gamekeeper; and the question of Trout *versus*
the Public has never yet been tried here. From
recent decisions of the Court of Session, it can
only be a trespass, after all, on uncultivated lands.
But such is the present observance, that before
you can go for a single afternoon's sport, even for
trout, you have to go through all the serfdom
and formality of *begging leave to fish*. The
present Lord Forbes of Castle Forbes, refused
this small favour to three gentlemen, who politely
asked his permission by letter to fish, where there
are plenty of trout and nothing to destroy.
While on the preservation of fish, I will observe,

that I can easily understand preserving trout, which remain stationary in streams and pools, but to preserve salmon, unless to be fished for the same day, is ridiculous, since they are constantly moving upward, and, in fact, seldom lie long in one place, and are always deteriorating in fresh water ; so the sooner they are fished out for food, the better. I have no hesitation in saying, the Don is as good a river for large trout as any in Scotland ;—indeed, for its length, I am inclined to think it is now the best. I never desired, nor do I care, neither is it generally to be wished, that a river should contain so many trout, as no skill is required for their capture. At every throw of the line were a trout to be taken, it would soon be quite sickening. What delight can that sportsman have who gets all his deer driven up to his tent in the hills, and he goes out and shoots them down in his morning gown and slippers—a regular *battue*—what delight can there be in being put into a preserve to shoot game, if, at every step you trod on a pheasant or a hare, and they could not get out of your way, and had no chance for their life ? This is a kind of sport which the true lover of it does not covet or desire. Fair play to all, the pursued and hunted, is the custom and the rule in every field where gentlemen meet. A certain amount of labour is desirable in the *rising* and the finding of game. The excitement of the sport is thus kept up ; and it greatly adds to the pleasure, when you do something in this way, that others fail in doing ; and we know no true sportsman would shoot a hare in its lair, or even sitting. In like manner, I only desire a fair stocked river of fish, with fair fishing therefor. I have little wish to be the *mere killer of many*, but rather, as the saying is, to have pleasure, not in the *prize*, but in the *pain*. We hear of some who kill 56 lbs. in a day. They have a greater desire to make themselves beasts of burden than I have ; and what is the use of loading an ass under such circumstances. No man, except of great strength, can fish in a May day comfortably with more on his back than twenty-five pounds weight ; and, as I always bag my own game, I seldom wish (indeed, it seldom happens) to have more than the half of this weight on any ordinary day I go forth. Many, many pleasant days has it been my privilege to enjoy myself by the water-side near Fintray. What were my feelings when I came down from pent up and

bustling *Babylon*, to the river Don, in April?—
How I inhaled the fresh and the pure air which
swept down from the Cabrach and Bennochie—
how delightful when the lark,—

> Bird of the wilderness,
> Blithesome and cumberless,
> Sweet be thy matin o'er moorland and lea.
> Emblem of happiness,
> Blest be thy dwelling place.
> Oh, to abide in the desert with thee !

How my heart was gladdened to see the yellow
water lily, giving early tokens of coming spring.
When I first put up my rod to begin, how delighted to see the primrose on the banks, and in
my paths near my favourite casts,—how cheer-
ing to see the busy mill—the never-closed gate
—and the hospitable fireside, where I had such
a sincere welcome ; and, should ever any of you
find yourselves in similar circumstances, I hope
you will feel as thankful in your heart as I had
cause to be ; and that while you wander by the
river side, you will silently and cheerfully give
your thoughts to the Giver of every tender mercy,
and not fail to remember all His benefits so
liberally bestowed on you.

Colquhonny,

In Strath Don, near Newe, the seat of Sir Charles
Forbes, is a good fishing place, and the inn is
pleasant and comfortable. I remember some
years ago being there with three others. We had
written the day before that we intended to come,
and I very well remember the morning we
arrived. The first thing we saw was Watson,
the innkeeper, carrying into the kitchen a very
fine whole carcase of a Highland wether. The
ride from Alford had given us all good appetites
to enjoy its loin, in the shape of capital chops, together with glorious reckin' porridge and cream.
On getting to our sport, we all of us fished
with fly. We found the trouts not quite so large
as farther down the river; but we all got a good
take of well-conditioned fish, although at the end
of March. The water, of course, is here not so
broad nor so heavy as lower down. We were
told that there was no difficulty in getting leave
to fish from its liberal proprietor. Near it is a
spacious hall or assembly room for the meeting
together of the neighbouring gentry and the
Clan Forbes, at balls or other festive occasions.

Alford.

This place is now easily reached by rail from Aberdeen, and the angler will find it a very pretty place. The inn is finely situated, overlooking the bridge ; and, indeed, you might cast your fly from the garden, which is between it and the river. There is water that may be fished near the town ; but, to fish much up or down toward Whitehaugh, I think you must obtain leave from the factors of the proprietors, who mostly live in Aberdeen, an introduction to whom, is not, I believe, difficult to obtain. The trout here are large and plentiful, and the water is good for partail and minnow, or Brown's phantom minnow, of Aberdeen, can be used with great success

in some of the rapid places, and you will seldom fail to hook large trout if the water is heavy or discoloured. Since this implement came into use, I have seldom failed with it, except when fishing the Tweed, the waters of which run much smoother and over a less rugged bottom, in most places where fish harbour, but neither in Tweed nor in Don do you need to throw it twice in the same place. If they do not seize it at its first visit, do not repeat it. Not so the partail, however; they will follow it and take it at the side, when you are recovering to pitch it forward again. There can be no doubt it is the smell that attracts them in this case, and also the real nature of the bait. They only dart once at the phantom, which they at once descry to be a substance having dangerous qualities. I have taken salmon with it both on Tweed and Don, but I would not like to affirm that they were clean ones. The phantom minnow may now be bought at the principal tackle shops in London. (It would be better named a *phantom smolt.*)

Castle Forbes.

I remember being here with three others, and beginning to fish below the Bridge of Keigh (I think it is called). We had amongst our take at the end of the day some trouts of 3 lbs. A very provoking incident occurred here. Three of us unfortunately took the north side of the river ; and, on coming to a place near a mill, we saw one friend on the opposite side getting grand sport, nearly every cast brought its victim to the fly, and we, anticipating wonders of course, began also, but found that we could not hook a single fin. The wind—a kind of north east, —blew right across the stream. The flies, drifting in a particular way to the other side, were eagerly sucked down as they floated toward the bank, and we had the mortifying satisfaction of seeing our friend fast filling his large pannier, when all that we took was scarce 2 lbs. apothecaries. The fly being cast from the other bank, against the wind, came back in so natural and peculiar a way, that the fish eagerly took them ; this is to be much studied in your fishings,—whatever side the wind blows to, there expect fish to lie. This is all a beautiful country, especially near the banks of the river, the course of which the eye can follow far, as it marks its way by the deeper green of the luxuriant foliage. This, on the whole, was a capital day's sport ; and, after dinner, like merry anglers, we chirruped over our cups ; the joyous jest and cheerful song went round, and I was called upon to sing the old ditty,—

It's when the apple tree it buds, it buds on every
   side,
And when the young men gae to woo, they're a
   busk'd up wi' pride,
They're a' busk'd up wi' pride, an' they mak'
   the shillings flee—
They gar the lasses weel believe they've lands
   and houses free.
But when that they are married, an' weel come
   to their sorrow,
The lands they are to buy, an' the shillings are
   to borrow.
Set them up in a reekie house, an' let them greet
   their fill.
If ye've brewed weel, my bonnie lass, ye'll drink
   the better yill!

Monymusk.

To lovers of Scotch strathspeys, this name will
recall one of the best of them. Here, having
obtained leave for a day's sport from the proprietor, we, of course, chose a day we thought
favourable for it, and three of us arrived at the
inn, Grant's, a little after breakfast, in rather a
cold day in the beginning of April. There is
a place called Paradise, a little above a mill,

which we were recommended to try, but one only of us went up to it. It fell to my lot; and I reached it by crossing a bridge, and coming down on the north side. I, in a short time, began opposite the one who got the south side, and soon saw that it was no go, as at one o'clock, I had scarcely got a trout. After this, however, I observed my friend and his boy pass downwards, and also noticed that the wind blew towards the south bank. I immediately repassed the bridge, and came on the same side of the water which the others, a little while before, had fished over, and left. I found better sport here, and soon began to feel the want of a boy, both to assist to take them off the hook and to carry the basket for me. I fished at this place for an hour, and then proceeded downwards to the inn, where we were to dine at 4.30. On getting to it, our several takes were weighed at a grocer's shop, and, in the basket which took up the water, was found 15 lbs. of fine trout (had also run a salmon),—24 lbs. in my own, and 27 in that of the other. In the 27 lbs. there were 4 dozen of trout,—in the 15 lbs., say 2½ dozen, but in the 24 lbs. basket, only 23 trouts. By one who had fished the Don from a child, it was admitted to·

be the best basket of yellow trouts he had ever
seen. There can be no doubt that there are
many smaller streams and burns, which supple-
ment the Don, and which would well repay the
angler, but, if permission is to be first asked and
obtained before you have leave to fish them,
why, is it not better to apply at once for the
larger favour? I never had any pleasure in
burn fishing, let the trouts be ever so large and
plenty, for who would *ploutter* in the Gady, or
others like it, if they could obtain the glorious
Don. I delight in a large stream and a good
extent of cast, and, as a rule, I should say,
especially in salmon fishing, those who can fling
out the most extent of line are those who do
best—say fifty feet from the top of the rod. It
stands to reason; they cover by far the widest
angle and extent of water fished. Salmon,
I should say, insist on the fly being given to
them in a particular way; you must throw it
beyond the middle of the stream, else there will
be little success with them. Their great temp-
tation is to see the fly swirl round, or come from
the bank over the middle of the stream; in
that case, you must throw a long line. Nearly
all the Don can be well commanded in this way,

as its run is deep, and not often overburdened
with trees.

> ' But a foot o' Don's worth twa o' Dee,
> Unless it be for fish and tree.'

Kemnay.

Here I have often fished, and know the streams
pretty well, and used to begin after a good strathspey on the fiddle, from the late schoolmaster.
When we appeared, the school at once had the
play for hours, and we found ere we were long
there, that we were not in a ' *Will ye hae
house,*' but in an inner chamber; all was provided and ready for us, consisting of cheese,
cakes, and a cauker (whisky); and on the fiddle,
to hear his Gregg's pipes, or the Reel of Tulloch,
was a great treat, and I have left his house with
a blythsomer and a lightsomer heart than when
I entered it. On leaving Kemnay, and coming
down to the river, you may pass over the water
until you get to the ' Breem Peel,' where once
' Broom bloomed fair to see.' This is a favourite
pool for both salmon and trout; indeed, this

water is famous for both. This is a pool that is
to the eye of an angler delightsome to see. On
the north side it is overhung with trees, which
afford a kind shade to the finny race ; and you
can so command it from the south side, there
needs no such switching as you are forced to
adopt in many good places. Switching may be
said to be a mode of casting the line, in order
not to strike the bank or any tree which is behind you. It is done by a peculiar turn and
jerk of the rod, never lifting all your line nor
fly off the water ; and you must either be able
to do this, or occasionally pass over otherwise
capital water. But it is not needed here, and
we pass down below the mill of Kemnay, the
stream of which, especially for grilses, is first
rate. Occasionally this flows in a rapid to near
the Gartless Pool, the first sight of which will,
doubtless, command your attention. I once killed
a grilse of 6 lbs. weight here ; and, leaving it on
the bank while I worked another in the upper
part of it, on returning to it I found that,
during my absence, an otter, which I observed
take to the water, had made his dinner off the
nape of the neck of my best fish, finding it,
no doubt, fresher than many an Alderman has

done, at a Lord Mayor's feast. I love the Gart-lees. There is a large piece of red granite lying at the top of the cast, shaped like an obelisk. One day while here, I suggested this for my monument, and asked my companion to indite me an epitaph. He immediately retorted the following :—

      ' *Donnez moi la paix.*'

Leaving this, we come down to Mr Gordon's of

Monar.

Capital water for both trout and salmon. Looking to the north, we see Aquhorthies, formerly a place for nuns, but now most happily done away with. Houlth, Rae Pot, and others quite as good, will always repay those who ply them. We come now to the celebrated Chapel Pool, for new run fish. Few better on Don. Would prefer to fish it from the south side, for you cannot from the north, without wading deep-ly into it. Many glorious runs of fish are often seen here ; and my lot has seldom been to pass it without seeing something exciting and heart-stirring to the angler. The water now abounds

with pools, and good ground for trout all the
way to Inverury. There are two or three pools
near Artannes, which should not be overlooked.
There is a capital inn at Inverury—no better in
Scotland—and great kindness is paid to wet-
footed and weary anglers.

Inverury.

About fifty years ago there was good salmon
fishing here. The rent of a good piece of water
was about £1 per year and the first clean fish;
but the cruives below Granholm were then open
three days a-week, and I know those still living
who killed their 40, and sometimes 50, lbs.
weight.

This is a convenient place to stop at. The
station faces the inn, and we have had experience of its comforts, both as regards its beds
and its dinners; and it is not very difficult to
obtain fishing, I believe, in this quarter, by applying to the innkeeper, Mr Annand of the
Kintore Arms.

I have fished in the Ury, which here joins the
Don; but, although it is said to be a good river

for trout, the party I was with did little or nothing as a *whole day's doings.*

Kintore.

We now approach this place, from which the Earls of the name take their title. Here, of late years, it is not preserved ; but in spring I have killed a good basket, fishing its upper parts. When you have a mild day and a gentle ripple on the different reaches of the river, you cannot doubt to have reward for your labour, if assiduously applied. Here we have also a railway station, and formerly there was a capital inn to rest and be thankful in, but it is now given up to that of Inverury. A long reach of uninteresting water, excepting some good places near Wester Fintray, until you come below Pitmedden. Here the Manse Pool for salmon has few equals. It is short but good, narrow but pithy, deep but silent. In the upper part there is pike ; in the middle, often new run salmon ; and at the lower we find foul and unclean fish and kelts. Then comes ' *Cothal Mills,*' to which I have alluded before, a spot endeared to me by many

fond recollections of its kind and hospitable
owners. This is capital fishing water for large
trout, and down to the splendid Coval Pot, where
there is both large trout and salmon. I may
mention, when fishing here, many a time and oft,
at the *end of the milltail* race, that during the
time the foul water was sent down from the
scouring tubs, I never could catch a trout,
although I have often tried to do so at the time ;
doubtless, they avoided this ' complication of
villanous smells,' compounded from soap and
various coloured dye stuffs, which has the effect,
I suppose, of giving them a *sair mouth ;* for, in
it, they do not bite ; and this puts me in mind
of an anecdote told me by a friend of mine,
who was present at the party :—In Shakspere
Square, Edinburgh, some forty years ago, lived
Lucky Johnston,—the famous Harry Johnston's
mother,—who kept an oyster shop. I remember
the name of *Pandores* being over the door in
great letters. One night during his engage-
ment at the theatre, she had invited a few of
her *cronies* to their supper; and, after the play,
to hear a funny story from *Maister Harry*, her
son. Well, they were all assembled, and Johnston came out with one of ' his very drollest ;'

the whole room was convulsed and in a roar, when an elderly dame, at the upper end of the room, rose up, and, making a curtsey, said, holding a kerchief to her cheek, ' *Maister Harry, you'll excuse me frae no laughing, for I hae got a sair mouth !'*

Parkhill.

Coval Pot, as it is called, is the first salmon pool on the estate of Mr Gordon ; and gentlemen of his acquaintance and neighbourhood, by subscribing to any good object of benevolence, or transmitting a small donation to him for such an object, will generally obtain leave to fish over his water, either for salmon or trout. The stream just above the forked ford, is one for trout, than which nothing could be more desirable, even in our fondest dreams of angling. On both sides you may, with his order, pursue your sport, saving below the bridge on the north side, opposite his mansion.

Fishing here is much changed from what it was formerly ; and so unsophisticated were the fish in *days of yore*, that for trout they fished

with four or five hairs to the fly ; and for salmon,
seven to the *tippet*. The yellow trout were often
as large in size as 7 lbs. ; and I have often
heard the story repeated by my late lamented
and respected friend, J. C., who was a keen
fisher then, that one afternoon he took one of
this weight, and, on expressing it to be of the
salmon kind, on showing it to Jock Bannerman,
he swore a great oath, and said, it was *only after
a'* but a yellow trout.

There can be but little doubt that another
cause of so much falling away of both kinds of
fish is the greater amount of fishing going on
now in nearly all our rivers than there used to
be in earlier days.   Look at the amount of
trouts, by a calculation that Mr Stewart lately
made, as relating to the Gala, 30,000 trouts
being fished from it every year (an amount, by
the by, I very much question), in fact they are
in every place 'ower muckle *hunted ;*' and all
salmon rivers, too, are much overfished with still
nets, wear short nets, and stake nets (see the
Duke of Richmond's evidence before the Com-
mittee of the House of Commons, on the last
Tweed Bill).

But to return to our muttons, as the French

say. Many who eat and who catch salmon cannot tell when they get a clean run fish. Many big (but long) fish are taken in spring, to all appearance clean and caller, but they are foul as sin—being fish that have spawned in the upper waters of Don. But while on this point, I am quite certain few, if any, Tweed fish ever repass Ashiestiel Bridge. When once they have passed that bourn to the spawning beds up the river, they may take a farewell of their salt element, for they never return to it. Not so on Don, at least, where I have now arrived. A great many fish pass down after spawning in the upper beds. The leister and other deadly weapons being decidedly less used against them, demoralising manufacturing towns being fewer on its banks ; the consequence is, we find hundreds of these in the pools of Don, if great floods have not already swept them away to the sea ; and I have seen us quite annoyed, while fishing for trout, by having all our small flies taken away by a motionless brute, which, by its sheer weight, went off with them. To the eye, I say they are silvery and white, but, on being boiled, they are soft and pale coloured in the flesh. These are known as kelts, or fish which have

spawned.[1] I have often killed fish of this kind ;
and many have I returned back, both on Don
and Tweed, which had the worm in their gills.
The fact is, that salmon are peculiarly constituted
and circumstanced, having, I may say, two
thorns in the flesh. In the sea they have a bug
or louse, which attacks them generally near the
vennal and pectoral fins; this drives them by
nature's law into fresh water, to get rid of it ;
and, when they stay long in fresh water, the
maggot comes into their gills, which drives them
again to seek the salt water, to get free of it.
Without both these elements, salmon cannot continue their species; and they may be said to live
continually between 'the devil and the deep sea.'

In proof of such fact, I may mention, that
sometime not long since, at a convivial meeting
of fishers, there happening to be a London friend
present, on the toast being drank, to the 'Lousy
Stranger,' he felt quite indignant, till it was ex-
plained. It only meant the clean run fish for
this sport. On another occasion, a gentleman
fisher came down in spring, and began to fish

[1] On Tweed they have what is called a mended kelt,
that is, a fish that has spawned early in the lower waters,
and has improved afterwards, before returning to the sea.

day after day. He was delighted with his sport and with his takes. A friend of mine—and few better in the knowledge of clean salmon—was invited to dine with this gentleman, and, on being introduced to him, accosted him thus,—

Friend.—Well, sir, I doubt you hinna had muckle sport.

Gent.—O, excellent, capital sport; I have killed nine or ten salmon.

Friend.—Are they clean?

Gent.—O, so beautiful and silvery, that I have sent five or six to my friends in England as presents.

Friend.—Guid be here! or, I'm a weaver! I should like to have seen them. I have fished till I'm sick, but can take nothing but foul kelts.

Gent.—O, I can gratify you in that, and forthwith took him to where they lay on ice—there they are, said he, as he held the light.

Friend.—Knapping his box, and taking a plentiful pinch of snuff,—In the name of '*Fresh cod!*' these are all as foul as the Man of Sin—with such presents he had persecuted his friends, not knowing better.

This reminds me of the great quantities of foul fish that were, for many seasons, sent from

Berwick to our French neighbours, and who ate them, no doubt, at the crack Palais Royal Restaurants, as 'saumon a l'Ecosse.' The trout-fisher cannot fail, ou a fine day, with gentle breezes, to obtain good sport on almost any part of the dead water, from Kintore to Fintray, and from which, for three or four miles there are many capital streams, where large trout are to be found 'at home ;' but they know little of creepers or May-fly fishing here, neither are they much skilled in the partail, in fact, it is an importation from the Tweed, and but very lately seen there. In early spring and in rapid places, no doubt, as I have said, Brown's phantom minnow is sometimes very killing. But fly is the best after all, for a long day's amusement, and you are less fatigued than with the other more laborious modes of capture.

I may mention a circumstance that occurred here about twelve years ago, and at a time, I believe, when a flood that carried away a part of the cruives, which are placed on the river a little above Old Aberdeen. I took five clean salmon out of the Manse Pool in one afternoon, and at the Coval Pool, two more in the evening ; and, curious enough, the whole five were caught through the upper jaw, as they all rose quite above the water in taking the fly. The three afternoons' sport yielded eleven new run fish, from 8 to 10 pounds each, and which had not been seen done for thirty years before.

While at the Don last spring, a rather funny circumstance occurred, showing better than much description, the difference of a Thames fisher from that of a Tweed or Don one. In Pitmedden Pool, at the upper part of it, there are large pike. One forenoon, my friend who was with me—for it is pleasant to hunt in pairs, —took the one end for them, while I took the bottom for salmon. After a *run* with one, I walked up to join him, and found him quietly seated on the bank, blowing a comfortable cloud, wanting only a bottle of stout to complete, while his rod was fixed and bending over the stream. His first recognition to me was,—Well, what have you done? Why, I have worked a fish these twenty minutes, and at last *he* fairly broke away, wishing me better luck next time ; and I am breathless and hot, and quite done up. But what have you been about? O, I am all right; I have one on. By all the fish pools in Heshbon, what do you mean? It's all right, I tell you—

don't you see how my line keeps sliding and
pirling out,—and in another minute he gave a
strike, enough to bring up a pig. Immediately he
was telegraphically connected to an enormous pike.

Banks of Donside, I owe thee much.

The Ythan.

This river I have fished, both at Newburgh and
Ellon, but with little success; at the latter place
I was annoyed by large foul salmon, and at the
former, I remember, we enjoyed the famous dish
of crappit heads, in company with the minister
of Foveran, whose company is equally good,
whether at a song, a strathspey, or a sermon.

The Doveran.

I have fished this river, beginning at Rothie-
may, now a very beautiful station on the Great
North of Scotland line to Inverness. The trout
are of splendid quality; and, when the river is in
order, will repay the angler with a full basket;
but liberty must be obtained. The proprietor is
the Earl of Fife, whom I know to be a very
kind-hearted nobleman. The day I and other

two went, we could only muster six or seven real minnows, every one of which, it was remarked, gained us a trout. The country is very fine, and, in the village, there is a good inn for refreshment. Here you may meet gentlemen in the full Highland garb, attended by their kilted gillies and others, and you at once imagine that you behold some of the great chieftians of the Isles—Sir Roderick M'Tavish, or Sir Reginald M'Lachlan—or some such, but, making inquiry, you find them sojourners from the great city, of *little* name and note, but when dressed in the Garb of old Gaul. It was in this quarter that friend Mill, after a summer's day of wading, was insisted on by the guid wife of the house where he was staying, that before sitting down to dinner she would bring him some water to wash his feet, as he had, she said, 'been in the dirty water all day.' 'What,' said he, 'my feet, and my heels even, are as clean and white as the skin of Gill Morris ; bring me a drink of whisky and I'd thank you rather.'

> Nae wonder, nae wonder, Gill Morris,
> My lady lo'ed thee weel.
> The fairest part of my bodie
> Is blacker than thy heel.

H

The Spey.

Those who are in this quarter, whether fishing or otherwise, should stop a while at Craigellachie. The Spey is decidedly like the Dee, purely a salmon river. They will find Jamie Shanks a capital fisher and guide on those waters, and some of the pools contain large clean fish; to run one and to kill it is a great feat. I know a gentleman who, a few years ago, killed one 26 lbs.; and, a few seasons ago, a friend of mine and a good fisher, hooked a fine fish, which went off with fly and every inch of his line, before you could say Jack Robinson. In such places, rod, line, and reel, must be strong and large, as the runs are very severe and exciting. For trout, it may be tried above the Iron Bridge, at Craigellachie, when the water is in good condition only. Their cast lines here as in Ireland, are usually made of whip cord, steeped in oil, and then, with a preparation of wax, etc., flies large, and with heron hackle.

LARGE SALMON FOUND ON SPEYSIDE.

Early one morning last week, Alexander

Grant, water-baliff, Grantown, found at Spey-side, near Skerryvore Pool, in Cromdale, a large male salmon. It was quite entire when found, with the exception of the right pectoral fin, which was scooped out by the root, the work evidently of an otter, from which we may fairly infer that this is the daintiest bit, in his estimation, while the smallness of the morsel indicates that the quality of the fish did not please; the under fins and tail were chafed and ragged, and the hook of the under jaw was very prominent. The fish was found on the *claddach*, two or three feet out of the water; it contained a few ounces of milt, and weighed 30 lbs.; its length was 4 feet 3 inches, girth at the thickest part 23 inches. These figures suggest what the monarch must have been some months ago, when, after the days of his purification were ended, he came up from the sea 'mighty as a giant refreshed with wine.' Our correspondent waxes warm with the idea :—

'What mad glee,' he says, 'must the restless creature have felt after his last annual refreshing baptism in the salt brine; and, as he felt home sickness coming on, have turned his tail to old Ocean, cleared the bar at Garmouth, and bravely cleaved the flood onwards, till he

bathed himself once more in the virgin waters of
his own loved native Spey. What dismay must
have travelled in his wake, what scrambling
among par and smolts and larger fry, rushing to
their hiding places, what sly peeping from under
large and little stones and shady banks, as the
mighty apparition—fat, firm, and 40 lbs (every
ounce of it, no doubt)—glided majestically by.
Pity that that accomplished veteran angler who,
some time ago, hooked and landed a 26-pounder
in these waters, did not engage him in the fray.
Such a capture would be worth chronicling.
Darting at the gaudy insect, his majesty of the
flood would soon learn that a poor, harmless
looking fly carried yet a very wicked sting in
its tail; but, not wishing to drown the poor
ephemeral, although it stung him, Mr Salmon
would leap with it high above the water, intend-
ing to let it there fly out of his mouth, but it
wouldn't go, and this feat would reveal to him,
oh, horror! that a strange land animal had him
in tow. Once, twice, and again, in quick suc-
cession, would he bound above the flood, probably to take the measure of his man, then,
turning his nose down the stream, he would run
as fast as his fins could carry him and the land-

drag would permit, and never slacken speed till
he reached Cromdale Boat Pool. Scarcely
would he halt in the deep water, there to take
breath, but off again for a second heat, leaving
the bonny " Haughs of Cromdale " far in the
rear. Though the combatants of the "Haughs"
should rise again, they could not frighten him
more than that solitary man on the shore, holding aloft a long enchanter's wand, and persever-
ingly haunting him like a ghost. Wouldn't the
juveniles of the flood, whom he so awed on his
upward journey, wonder what was up with him
now, and laugh in their sleeves (if they had any)
to see him stupidly fumbling about, and thus led
like a bullock to the slaughter. What telegrams
would run along that gossamer line of communication between man and fish ? what doubts, and
fears, and hopes, and heart-tremors would be
there ere the retiring sun should witness the tug
of war going on languidly, but still doubtfully,
near the low-lying haughs of Dalvey? Nor
would it be any shame to the monarch of the
flood, after battling so long and so valiantly,
there to quit his native dominions, and lie lowly
at the foot of the conqueror, acknowledging his
supremacy, and there, on the daisy-fringed

bank, near the old ash trees, to heave his last gasp, while the long slanting sunbeams gilded his gorgeous garniture of silvery scales. Meet termination this to his reign; fit deathbed, too, for the hero of a hundred fights, whether by flood or field. But to be found on a bleak December morning, lying long and lank on the strand, as if his own pure native Spey had rejected him, the glorious glitter of his scaly vesture dimmed, his symmetry nowhere, his fins ragged —looking the very ghost of what he was—and a gash in his throat, suggesting that want made the miserable creature commit suicide by running himself against some sharp root stump in the river bank—that surely was a most ignominious end!'

Elgin.

The beautiful ruin, the Cathedral, attracts many visitors, and is well worth a visit. A curious story is connected with it. Gullian, a beggar and her son, lived here for years among the ruins; and how the same son, after making· his fortune in India, returned to his native place, and bestowed so much to build schools, and endow them. The Lossie you may pass, unless in flood.

The River Ness.

Let's have three days of rain on the hills of Glengary,
Then a gentle west wind, and by jove I'll be merry.
The war-cry shall be—'rod, line, boots, and reel.'
Two hours on the water will make a full creel.

No Cockney, or Frenchman, or 'anglers from Wales,'
Will do on the Ness, tho' their 'parrs' are all whales;
But waist-deep in rapid, or pool, you must stand,
It will ne'er do to fish the old Ness from the land.

Then steadily walk into Macintyre's Pool,
With a switch, and a whack, send out thirty yards full;
A good "*Saturday fly*" will soon get you a rise;
Cast again, and an Alderman grilse is your prize.

What angler has not heard of the fame of this
river in times past; but, from causes unknown,
of late years there has been comparatively little
done in it. For some time it was rented by a
number of gentlemen, who formed themselves
into a club. In 1858 I became one of them,
and went to Inverness, expecting to see wonders
done. The seasons had been moderate before,
and great was the sport looked for; but, although
after a nice flood in the river, and the weather
almost everything that could be desired; and,

after a stay of a fortnight or three weeks, I found, as in most places where fishing is the question, that little was to be done ; and, up to the close of the season, the same result succeeded. There was little or no fishing for salmon in the Ness, that year, with the rod. The consequence was, that we betook ourselves to trout, and we had some very good sport on a small loch, about seven miles from Inverness,—Loch Ashtie, I believe, but it must be fished with a boat, which Mr D. N——l, with genuine hospitality, sent up over night, in a cart, for our accommodation. We found numbers of trout, and some of good size, say 1½ lbs. The angling not being good, we had more time to spend, and we were much gratified with visits to the fall of Foyers, and also to those of Kilmorack. On returning, we saw one or two poachers plying their vocation with the otter. This consists of a piece of wood, about two feet long, and about an inch-and-a-half thick, leaded or keeled at bottom. Two pieces of cord are then inserted at the side, *fore* and *aft*. A triangle will thus be formed, say two feet in length. To this you join a good cord line, communicating, of course, with your reel, or attached to the but-end of your salmon rod ; it follows, as a matter of course, that if you put this in the stream, the force of it acting on its side will propel it to the other side of the river, thus :

And you attach to your line five or six hooks, or more, the length of their respective lines, shortening as they recede from the rod. When a fish takes any of the flies, you pull him in to your side, or, *vice versa*. Raking or harrowing the water is different from this, and is practised on both Tweed and Don, thus : Two rods— generally strong ones—are procured—the lines run out according to width of the river. The ends of both are joined together, thus :

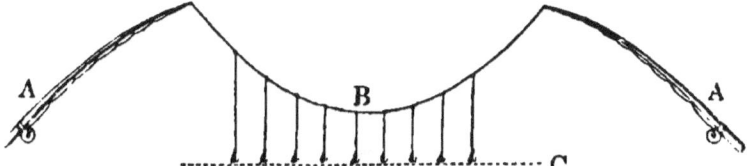

A the rods. B the flies, and C the water.

You then harrow or drag them up or down the stream—generally up; if a fish takes on

your side, you drag him, forthwith, to you;
and if, on the other, you let out line, so as your
opposite rod may take him to his side. But they
can only be called *pot wallopers* who have re-
course to such methods—no true angler adopts
them. The Ness was, last year, taken by a
gentleman, of bitter beer notoriety; and it has
been rather a bitter draught to those gentlemen
who have fished here for so long a time, to find
their occupation gone, by the heavy purse
from John Barleycorn. As a trouting river, I
should say, by what I saw Mr Lowe do in it, it
is not worth much, as the best fishers find them
' few and far between.' The doctor is a good
salmon fly; and I have heard of seventeen fish
being all killed with one, while it was nearly all
worn to the iron. As an illustration, that while
they are in the humour, salmon will rise and
take anything, a few seasons ago, a friend of
mine captured here two or three fish, with the
thumb of an old kid glove, stuck on a plain hook.[1]

[1] The angling club, with truly piscatorial perseverance,
have again leased the lower part of the river; the
gentleman above alluded to being one of them.—*Letter
from Mr Nicol*, 23d January 1860.

Inverness

IS, I believe, the farthest point that Cromwell went. He gave them the cabbage plant and the English tongue; for, they say, they speak the language here better than any other town in Scotland; still there is a little TWANG of the Gaelic accent with it. In the months of tree foliage, I should advise all tourists to walk out a mile, and view the river, and especially from Campfield, where, no doubt, those lines of C. Mackay, well suggest themselves :—

> Ye happy, happy trees,
> That in perpetual ease
> Stand on the soil where ye as saplings grew,—
> That lift your branches fair
> To the embracing air,
> And feed on sunshine, rain, and morning dew,
> I would that I could lead,
> In all my thought and deed,
> A life, ye happy trees, as beautiful as you.

A very good view of the town has lately been taken from this very spot, by an eminent artist. Now, it is often observed by those who are no fishers, that there is nothing new in it; the

same thing over and over again and again ; but,
I tell you, there is constantly something new
occurring. Lowe, who can draw a long bow
with any man in Scotland,—but only on the
fiddle—assured me that, a few years ago, he
hooked a fish in the Ness, and it at once run out
all his line. He did not like to break it, and, of
course, the worst came to the worst ; for he threw
after it rod, reel, and line, and trusted to Providence, like an honest angler, for their restoration.
However, on getting below the tree, and on
searching the pool, no fishing-rod could be re-
covered or seen, after two hours fruitlessly
spent looking for it. His son was dispatched for
grappling irons ; and, after a good deal of toil,
they succeeded in finding the rod, and, on re-
suming it and winding up,—never thinking of
a fish—to their great surprise a fine new run
grilse of 9 lbs. still held the hook, which, after
a little play, they landed and bagged, to the
great satisfaction and surprise of both.[1]   He is

[1] An honest farmer who often returned from market
top-heavy, had heard his guidwife say—' When in any
difficulty, just put your trust in Providence.' One night
coming home, he fell off his horse, and he made several
unsuccessful attempts to get on. At last, for about five

free to confess, that if there had been no fish when he wound up his line, he would have, to the day he died, said, that he had hooked a twenty pounder, so lively and lightning-like was the run of it. The Ness is one of those rivers, that, unless after very great rains, flows on in a pure and constant stream, from one of those fountains which does not send forth sweet water and bitter at the same place, its source being from a loch of considerable magnitude, twenty-six miles in length, and a mile and a-half in breadth, and, like a well-regulated mind, it is not easily disturbed. It takes a great deal to rouse her; she often, like the good housewife, wears the green spectacles, and sees and hears much around her, heeding it not. Much rain may fall on the distant straths and glens, before it makes any impression on her smooth and smiling face; so that her run is uniform and pellucid. O, that all our minds generally flowed on as clear and calm

‘ As this shining river, or e’er it reached the sea.’

It has good pools for salmon near the loch, and

minutes, he silently recommended himself to its power; then giving a spring up, he went clean over on the other side of his horse altogether, with—Hoot—hoot, Mr Providence; when *you do, you overdo !*

also on Lord Salton's water; but the Red Braes, and M'Intyre's Pool are the best on the lower part of it. On the last days of fishing for the season, there are some ludicrous scenes to be witnessed here—so many taking their farewell casts—in broken rods, fouled lines, and wet jackets. The town is much improved of late, by the new suspension bridge, the old stone one having been swept away by a great flood some years ago; it is an object of interest to the stranger. At the castle, from which there is a fine view, there are a Russian gun or two from Sebastopol.

> Ta Hielan' hills pe high, high, high,
>> Ta Hielan' hills pe lang.
> But then my friends, keep aye in mind
>> Ta Hielan' whisky strang.
>>> Ta Hielan' whisky strang.

> And when she will pe for to go to the hill,
>> She'll no care though its lang;
> For in her cheek one Hielan' gill
>> Will make her very strang.
>>> Will make her very strang.

> She'll no say she be tooked twa,
>> And may be she'll took three;

But what suppose she tooked six,
What pusiness you or me?
What pusiness you or me?

A gentleman one morning said to his gilly, 'You are drunk you rascal.' 'Praise pe plessed for it I am not, but I wish I was,' was his reply.

Findhorn.

Freeburn, about 18 miles from Inverness, can be easily reached by coach every morning about 6. This is a nice and comfortable inn, at which the coach changes horses, kept by M'Intyre, who combines with it a little farm. Here you are only a few minutes from your work, which is a great convenience; for, if you should go first up the river, three or four miles above, you can fish downwards to your inn; and if you go a few miles downwards you can fish up to it. There is no long walk, unless you order it so, when you leave off your vocation. Last year I was there with a friend, and we had good sport. I found they did not take the fly very readily (August), and we plied them with the partail and phantom minnow. The

partail was best, as I have stated before; they
may renew the charge at it, but they seldom or
never do so to the phantom. We found many
trout of 2 lbs., and some of the most beautiful
'yellow guinea colour' and 'bonniely bedropp'd
wi' crimson hail' than any I ever saw in Tweed,
and when so, in the most desirable condition. It
abounds with many rapid streams, so suitable for
the playing of this bait, and I do not think it is
much fished here. Its channels give indications
of a roaring flood or spates, occasionally, which,
I am told come so rapid that the angler is often
in great danger from the suddenness of its
approach. Both days we got baskets of good large
trout. I did not hear, while there, that any
permission was required, probably the innkeeper
has the privilege for those who take up their
quarters with him. We always took out our
lunch with us, and dined on returning, at 6 or 7
o'clock. As a good rule for all fishers, I would
recommend the advice of my old friend, Mrs
Hardy,—' When you go out to fish, tak' a bit
in your pouch, for you can tak' a drink o' the
burn, but you canna tak' a bite o' the brae.'

I was much gratified each evening, after the
coach passed about 9, to hear family worship

in this rather forlorn place—M'Intosh, in a loud stentorian voice, reading out in couplets the lines of the Psalm, in the same continuous strain of the key note of the tune (Colshill) they were singing. It put me in mind of the old Covenanters, and it was quite refreshing to hear a family lifting up their song of praise to their heavenly Father after their toils and before retiring to rest. It brought to my mind the Cottar's Saturday Night, which, to this day, I can never read without shedding tears, for it kindles such joy and delight in the heart. I would refer particularly to the verses following —this graphic description and picture of Scottish rural life—

> ' The cheerfu' supper done, wi' serious face,
> They round the ingle form a circle wide ;
> The sire turns o'er, wi' patriarchal grace,
> The big ha' Bible, ance his father's pride.
> His bonnet reverently is laid aside,
> His lyart haffets wearing thin and bare ;
> Those strains that once did sweet in Zion glide,
> He wales a portion wi' judicious care ;
> And " Let us worship God ! " he says, with solemn air.'

I am glad to say that there are many families among the peasantry of Scotland who exercise their households thus, not only on Saturday nights but on every evening of the week—may their race never cease out of the land we live in!

A week could be spent very nicely here in the spring, when, I am told, the trout fishing is excellent with the flies, the same as are used on Don

FISHING RIVERS.

The Tay,

WHICH flows from Loch Tay, sends the largest quota of water to the ocean, of any river in Great Britain. I have fished up at the Falls of the Tummel and the Garry, near Blair Athol, but never with what you might call success; neither while there did I see anything done by others. In July, they say, many sea trouts and grilses are taken here after floods. There is an excellent inn at Pitlochrie, which is a very pretty village to live at, the celebrated Pass of Killicrankie being near. We were also informed that there were capital takes of trout got in Loch Broom, in the neighbourhood, and if the angler extends his journey and make his way to Loch Rannoch, a distance of some miles, Tighnalinn inn, at the head of it, will be found to be very fair quarters, and liberty to fish is soon obtained from Robertson of Struan. There are good trout, some of large size, got here by trolling, to the size of 15 lbs.

Stanley.

I once sojourned here for a week. It is five or six miles from Perth northwards; was much delighted with its situation and our quarters, in a small inn at the end of the village, near to the large spinning-mills. Nearly all the young population are employed in the spinning-mills, and at early morn the rest of all and sundry is unceremoniously broken at five o'clock, by the blowing of a horn from the centre of the place —and very delightful it is to see so many going so early to their daily occupations. There are some capital pools for fish both up and down here. We had the use of a boat while we fished above the Linn of Campsie, a rugged basaltic dyke, which crossed the river at this place, and is the scene where Wull o' the Wyde, in the Fair Maid of Perth, leapt across when he made his escape. The river, when I was there, was low, as I waded across with ease about half-a-mile above this Fall.

We hooked large salmon both above and below this, but, owing to the ruggedness of the bed, we often lost them, the line fixing between stones lying against each other through which the fish ran and broke our line or hook, which we had the provoking satisfaction of witnessing two or three times.[1] The river, at this part, is interesting and beautiful, and we often got into situations which the wader's eye can only be gratified with ; and had we been proficients in sketching, how many delightful neuks of scenery could we have gratified our friends at home with. In this respect fishing has its pleasures. While we wade, we often bring ourselves into parts that have been seldom seen from such

[1] Duchar, the smith, told us the following story, which took place here. Three young gentlemen came to fish, and, like all Londoners, were well provided with all sorts of tackle ; but salmon, being their chief end, were recommended and put under his instructions. He took them to that fine stream below the mills, and they were not long in hooking a good sized grilse. After playing it for some time, one of them, who had a span new cleek or gaff, was told to gaff it when it came near the side. In vain he tried to do so, at last the smith asked him what he was fumbling about? He innocently observed, that 'if it did not open its mouth how could he gaff it;' which caused a good laugh at his expense, you may be sure.

points of view, 'tis good therefore to combine both accomplishments. The mere killing fish may tire you in time, but the landscape and picturesque rocks, never,

> Ever charming ever new,
> When will the landscape tire the view?
>
> *Dyer.*

Having now gone over most places I have fished in Scotland these last twenty-five years, I must yet add another place whither I went about eighteen years ago with a friend. I believe it is in Argyleshire and not far from Ardnamurchan, say twenty miles from Fort William. If it happens that you desire to go there, you must make your way to Glasgow, of course were you at Inverness or Elgin, you would go *via* Caledonian Canal. The steamer leaves the Broomielaw early in the morning, and you get to Fort William that evening; here you must rest and proceed on hire or on foot, as we did. After ferrying over the Lochy, I believe you proceed along Loch Eil,—on the road pay a tribute to the memory of that gallant man, Colonel John Cameron of the 92d Regiment, who fell at Quatre Bras in 1815, you will see his monument as you go, on the right hand near

Fassifern. Continuing up the north side of the Loch, all at once Loch Shiel opens to view. You are now at the upper end, and where the Pretender was met by the Clan Cameron, a monument to whom, a M'Donald of Glenalladale has erected at his own expense. It is a fine object to see the figure looking down the Loch in such solitude. You are now at Glenfinnan inn. We fished that evening on the Loch, near the statue of Charles Edward; but the fishing we came to try was over the hill.

Loch Eylt.

This lies about four or five miles from the Glenfinnan inn, and is fished with boats. We wind our way up a glen. In going up this glen you will observe two beautiful *sandstone dykes*, in a ridge of high rocks on the right hand, the remains of some great forest, as is seen by the many decayed roots of the oak and fir trees, —one huge stump of the monarch of the wood stands yet here, and life is not yet extinct, tho' all its

'Youthful companions are faded and gone.'

What appears once to have been a hamlet is also quite levelled, the happy inmates now perhaps in Canada, yet it still continues to look on, speaking in 'silent eloquence' to those who direct their steps to its roots. I often ran down from the path to visit it ; could it have spoken, it might have discoursed of Ossian and Fingal. The road now turns in the direction of the Island of Egg,— the great attraction of geologists,—and we soon come in sight of two or three little lochs in connection with one another; in fact, I saw a shepherd wade through to the opposite side, between two of them. A burn now runs the opposite way to the one we came up by, and which, in spawning time, is filled with salmon and sea trout. I wish I could interest you in this place, so

'Far removed from noise and smoke.'

In these lochs, the property of Lord Cranstone, you have great variety of fish. The days varied, sometimes we had 50 to 60 sea trout, from 1 lb. to 2 lbs. each. We generally were driven there, and the horse grazed about till it was time to get home to dinner : this was about the end of July. The yellow trout did not favour us much with their company, probably fishing with too large a fly; on some days we numbered a couple of grilses, and we caught lots of finnocks, and one day we had two beautiful char, the size of a half pound. This is a handsome shaped fish of a deep crimson colour. The boat, man, and horse and cart, cost about 7s. 6d. per day, by which means we were not fatigued going or coming. There is a small island on which we used to do our fish in a conjuror—a little round shaped tin stew pan, with lamp heated by strong whisky or spirits of wine,—done in this way, with a little pepper and salt, finnocks especially, and also other fish, never can taste better—fresh air and hunger being their best sauce. All the time we fished here we used nothing but the fly: it is said char do not take it, but we found it otherwise in Moidart and Glenalladale. And, I again beg to observe, that there were no particular flies used but the common trout or loch flies;—all the while, they took sometimes one sometimes the other.

In the interval of all these different periods of time, I have occasionally gone to places near London; for instance, I have been at West Drayton, the sign of the 'Trout,' when *old* Parr kept it. This was about 1823. The water fished

in there was little worth after Cockneys came
down on the Saturday evening, and used to fish
on the *Sunday*, a thing which, I may say, I
never did. They took dace, roach, and perch ;
but, it was small fishing to me. I fished farther down below the mill ; but at one time a
great many years after, I took only one small
trout. I have, when October was a fine month,
taken a dozen or two of other fish, dace, etc.,
but it was more a run for fresh air than
any other thing. Hubert de Burgh, Esq., is
the Lord of the Manor here ; and, to him, I
was indebted for leave to fish. It fell off
for many years ; but I chanced to walk here
about a year ago, and I saw the fruits of preserving water ; there were then plenty of fine
large trout, but I was told few could take them
with rod and line ; many of these were four and
five pounds weight, and I hope again to try
my hand on them some of these days shortly.—
For the sake of recreation, I have also gone to

𝔐𝔞𝔦𝔡𝔢𝔫𝔥𝔢𝔞𝔡,

And fished just behind Lord Orkney's, with little success. I must confess I never saw, all the times I was there, more than two or three trout, say, three-quarters of a pound, taken with the fly. I have taken chub with fly, under the bushes, a little above ; and I have seen some of my friends, apparently good fishers, try all day at the Wear, and come off in the evening, without getting an offer : and, the last excursion to the same place, with other four, we never saw a fin. I have also fished from a boat, below the bridge and about Bray, with little better success, although my friend, who accompanied me, took, I think, a brace of jacks about 3 lbs. each, after losing, I should say, in traces and hooks, on the weeds, nearly the worth of twenty shillings ; but I never yet fished from a punt in the Thames, with all the well known appendages of ease and comfort which we so often see indulged in at Richmond and Twicken-ham.

The Uske.

In coaching days I have also gone to the
Uske, in Monmouthshire ; and when I had persevered for two days at the salmon, I was told,
on my return, 'to take mine ease in mine inn,'
for the very day previous to my coming, all
the pools had been swept out by the nets—this
was the beginning of September.

Farningham

ON THE DARENT (KENT).

I went to this a few years ago, with a friend,
who insisted to take my double-handed rod.
We went, but he never put it up ; I, however,
persevered, and got four trout, which the people
at the inn said was quite *a take;* and unless,
you fish in the preserved waters of Sir Thomas
Dyke, Bart., you seldom did more.   They
were the prettiest trout I have ever seen ; so
small in the head and so beautifully 'be-dropped
wi' crimson hail.'   You soon get to this place
by the rail from London Bridge, then per coach

some four or five miles—distance from town, seventeen miles.

Carshalton-on-the-Wandle.

Near Croydon is a famous fishing place, but so *preserved* and *clubbed*, that you cannot get a line thrown on its streams, unless you are introduced by a member. I have, some years ago, got some good trout; but, I am afraid, it may be said as it has been said of the Fifeshire rivers, 'the *dulcia* of the angler having vanished before the *utilia* of the community.' Paper and printing-mills are doing their work here also.

The Mole

(LEATHERHEAD).

It is an age, I may safely say, since I cast a fly on the waters of Mr Hankey of Fitcham-park. The country all around this place is beautiful in May and June. I remember, it was the early hay-making, and, although it was a good day, I did little; and the gentlemen themselves, although out also nearly all the day, only took one trout, about one pound; but how pleasant it was to drink a horn of good old ale and enjoy a good luncheon,—which they very kindly invited me to,—by this very bonnie stream; and, as I never fished in it but once, I cannot speak of its capabilities as a trouting river, at this place. My whole theory, however, is, that one small fly does as well as another; but when you have a mind to try any of these streams near the great City, your best plan decidedly is, to put yourself in communication with some intelligent person who has fished there; or, apply to some tackle-maker in the neighbourhood where you intend to go; or, to buy from some of those well known makers in town, whom I have already named, and who dress them now so neatly on such fine gut, that the olden time fishers had no idea of in the days of ' old Isaak, and his friend C. Cotton.'

North Wales—Betty's-y-Coed.

The Conway is a considerable river at this place, but the trout fishing is not worth going

to in the months of August and September—at
this time there are some sea trout, a good many
about three-quarters of a pound, and although
there are salmon, which are fished for very assiduously, I never saw one taken by the rod the
whole time I was here. There is a net fishing
at the bridge of the Caldron—Pont-y-pain,—
about two miles up the river, and, after a flood,
they occasionally take two or three of a morning,
below the salmon leap, beneath the bridge. I
was told there are often large fish here late in
the year. You are obliged to pay about 8s.
per day for your fishing. I declined to do so
till I saw some others get sport—this, however,
was so meagre, that I did not put up my salmon
rod, and, even when I went a good way up the
river, I could make little of the trout. I also
tried other rivers in the vicinity, Llugwy, etc.,
and had no better success—one is much amused
by seeing all the appendages of a salmon fisher
—rod, flies twisted round the hat, wading boots
and gaff, borne along by many a fine youth;
but, in the evening, it was generally all in vain.
The scenery all about this part is well worth
notice, and it seems a favourite place of resort
for artists, who are found ensconced in every

corner where there is an interesting view to be
obtained. There is also a lake up among the
hills, about three miles from this, where the
salmo-ferox is sometimes caught; but, although
I tried it twice, with all kinds of flies and partail, I could not even obtain a rise or an offer.
At the Waterloo Inn (William's), near the Iron
Bridge of the same name, you can have good
quarters as a fishing place, and at moderate
charges. The Falls of the Conway and the
Swallow Falls, are interesting. The proprietor
is Lord Willoughby dé Eresby.

The Ahr

(GERMANY).

This river, the valley of which is so celebrated for its picturesque scenery, is about
eighteen miles from Bonn, on the Rhine. The
finest part of it is, certainly, at a small village,
Altenahr, situated quite close to the river, the
rocks from its sides rise in some places nearly
300 feet perpendicularly—the view from the
old castle—the turnings and windings of the
river make it altogether a most interesting place.

The people are mostly in humble circumstances of life, living by the cultivation of the vine. The valley of the Ahr being far-famed for the rich Ahrweiler wine, which place lies farther down, towards the Rhine. I wished much to try this stream, having brought reels and flies, but no rod, never doubting, that in a place like Bonn, I could easily procure one. In this I was woefully disappointed. All I could find was a very sorry one, at a perfumer's; it might have been said to resemble Aaron's rod (though only a walking-stick), for it had swallowed up all the others of its kind in the place; so, after a deal of tying and fixing, I succeeded in putting it together; but, at almost every throw, it went out at the ferrules, which were only made to hold together after the wood swelled by moisture. I found lots of grayling, and the river did not run heavier than the Gala, at Stow. They took the fly freely; but I never liked this fish, they bleed so at the mouth when hooked. Seeing there were trout, I began next day, and was surprised when I took two or three smolts. I soon, therefore, had partail; and I killed, in the rapid places, trouts of 3 lbs., and also other kinds of fish. We were much amused at seeing some of the villagers turning out to see us fishing with the rod and line—a thing seldom witnessed by them,—their usual mode of doing so is by net, or trap rather, which they set in different runs of the river. It reminded me very much of the Welsh rivers; no doubt, exposed to great spates and *overfloodings*. After heavy rains, it was also difficult, as in Wales, to get at places, from stone embankments, toward which the stream often ran deeply. This was in the month of August. On returning to the inn, we learned that in October and November large salmon came up from the Rhine, and that they took them by the spear, etc.; and they said that the fishing was good in spring time. The inn was a very good one in 1857,—a good large room below, although the bed-rooms had little comfort; and I learned that the expenses here were moderate, if you agreed for a time. It is, altogether, a most delightful country; and, we were told, that better streams and rivers were eight or nine miles further off; but, not being well accoutred, we did not think it wise to visit them.

Norway.

Those who have visited this country have given me no great idea of their doings ; and the accommodation is only 'tolerable, and not to be endured ;' bad beds and bad living, boatmen, and great rough water, yarn lines like ropes, and large flies. I have read of great things here ; but, although I have spoken to many gentlemen who have fished, they never gave me such a description, that I much desired to follow. Sir John Lees read me the other day part of a letter, giving an account of a gentleman who hooked a salmon in one of its rivers at five o'clock in the evening, and, after working it all night, was so worn out at six o'clock next morning, he was *quite done out*, that he gave his rod to a friend, who *lost the fish in five minutes !*

Now, as a general rule (and to know when to follow them, and when to depart from them), for salmon, doubtless, the angler's highest sport, as showing his dexterity, you are to cast your line 'fine and far off,' and always at a great angle, and as far to the other side as you possibly can throw, so as to let your fly sweep round, as he, in most

cases, takes it at the side you are on, or when you
let your fly first fall—as you never fish up the
water for him, and I consider a long line indispen-
sable, as he is a very timid fish; although I have
seen them follow and take the worm in the latter
end of the season, when the river was small, at my
very feet. For trout, a long line, too, but cast
right across the river, and you often take more
fish the moment your fly alights on the water,
than when you drag or '*harrle*' your flies round
for another cast. Some of the most successful
fishers seldom move the point of their rod much,
others again play it a good deal, and with as much
success. In this way, you observe the fish when
they rise (and it is a beautiful sight to see the
salmon do so), but I have taken more large trout
when the fly was sunk under the water. Do not
stay in endeavouring to entice a trout, as it seldom
rises twice. I have, on the other hand, seen a
salmon enticed, so that he has risen six or seven
times, and then take it at last. This is, no doubt,
rare; and, on the contrary, as many times they
rise and do not take the hook, which is called '*grip-
ping slack.*' Now, instead of carrying all kinds
of feathers, as I have said before, to busk hooks,
the best way, in these days of cheap postage and

speed, is to send to those you know make them, either in town or country. I prefer to buy them near the localities I am about to fish, march dun, dothril, hare's lug dun, and black palmer, these, of course, on different sizes. With these I would set off to fish almost anywhere. I have seen changes of flies answer, while others who continued the sport without any change do equally well on the whole day, there being atmospherical changes during which no fish will look up ; and again, there are hours of feeding, in which they will snap and take anything and colour of fly. The study of where fish lie, and the places to be at a certain time of day, are most important things to every angler, and never is an old rule more exemplified than in this case, that

Experientia docet.

And now, I would leave off, and affectionately recommend you to pursue this healthy exercise at any spare time you may have, from March to September. How delightful to find yourself on the bank of some beautiful river, your spirits and hilarity flowing with cheerfulness, and your mind not corroded with the cares of life,—' not slothful in business,' having been the Christian maxim of your life, with honesty of purpose and straight-forwardness, with a gracious and a smiling countenance, 'do to others, what you would that they should do to you.' If you are in robust health, rejoice in Him who hath bestowed such a blessing, and do not forget to think of those who cannot enjoy it, or who cannot spare the time. If you feel weak, be thankful you are still spared to recruit yourself, and forget not the many who, from weakness of bodily strength, cannot be partakers of your pleasures. Commend yourself at all times to the great Giver of all good; enjoy yourself in these, and let your heart cheer you; but, know, for all this, God will bring you into judgment.

NOTE.

THE DUKE OF ROXBURGH ACT FOR 1859.

The rod-fishing ends 30th November and begins first day of February. No cleek to be used from 15th September to 1st of May, and to fish with no baits but artificial fly only. Net fishing closes 14th September; after this, if there are floods, the salmon-fishing has now a chance to be good. We have no fish to speak of in the upper waters. If the river is low, and above the Ettrick to Peebles, there are seldom many fish until after two or three floods; in fact, to bring them into *these* waters, the river must be heavy for a fortnight or three weeks. After a heavy flood, or even two, it requires one or two small floods to make anything like salmon-fishing. These twenty-five years, the fishing has been gradually falling off. What this new Bill will do remains to be seen. The present season just over has not been good. Few were caught by rod and line in these upper waters, although there were two floods in October and also middle of November. The fish appear not to have got to the upper waters by the 30th of November, viz., *the day of closing.*

CLOSE OF SALMON ROD FISHING ON TWEED.—By the Duke of Roxburgh's Act, these fishings ended on the 30th ult.—on the whole, a bad season. Below Kelso fish were plentiful; but in the upper waters—say, above Yair Bridge—the fly-fishing was decidedly poor indeed. Mr Locke, of Regent Street, captured a good fish of 23 lbs. after a severe run of upwards of two hours.—*Court Journal,* 3*d December* 1859.

In regard to trout-fishing, the new Bill should provide for this also. That there should be a close time for them is much to be desired. Few people care for fishing for these after October, as they are decidedly out of season till March. But if there were no fishing, say from November to March, as is the case in Ireland ; also, to have a license for salmon-fishing ; for trout, it would be the means of preserving many a salmon, and many a redd, as poachers would then be known who go now to the river under pretence of fishing for trout, when it is all the while to exercise their calling for salmon—

'He came for draff, but drink was his errand.'

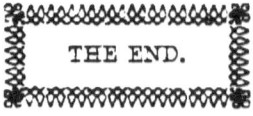

THE END.

MURRAY AND GIBB, PRINTERS, EDINBURGH.